Capture and Redemption

Third in a Series of Novels
of the French and Indian War

Brenton C. Kemmer

FIRESIDE FICTION
2007

FIRESIDE FICTION
AN IMPRINT OF HERITAGE BOOKS, INC.

Books, CDs, and more—Worldwide

For our listing of thousands of titles see our website
at
www.HeritageBooks.com

Published 2007 by
HERITAGE BOOKS, INC.
Publishing Division
65 East Main Street
Westminster, Maryland 21157-5026

Other books by Brenton C. Kemmer:

Redcoats, Yankees, and Allies:
A History of Uniforms, Clothing, and Gear of the British Army
in the Lake George-Lake Champlain Corridor, 1755-1760

Freemen, Freeholders and Citizen Soldiers:
An Organizational History of Colonel Jonathan Bagley's Regiment, 1755-1760

So, Ye Want to be a Reenactor? A Living History Handbook
Brenton C. Kemmer and Karen L. Kemmer

War, Hell and Honor: A Novel of the French and Indian War

The Partisans: Second in a Series of Novels of the French and Indian War

International Standard Book Number: 978-0-7884-4452-4

SACRIFICE & FAMILY

It was a chilly morn in March 1757 when Charles Nurse began to stir. He could hear the wind howling through the clapboards of the attic above; he could feel the warmth of the body beside him.

As his eyes began to peer open, Charles rolled over and put his arms around his wife.

"Good morning," whispered Charles as his lips found hers.

"Good morning, my husband," she replied.

Mary Elizabeth began to stretch and rub her eyes. Charles moved his hand to her stomach and felt for movement.

They had wed in November upon Charles' return from the army. Their love now was producing a child, and the two of them could not be filled with more joy and excitement.

Mary rolled off the rope bed and let out a soft yelp as her feet hit the rough, cold, pine plank floor. She slipped into a pair of soft brocade slippers Charles had purchased for her for a wedding present. She then pulled a long, woolen, green robe over her linen shift and left the bedchamber. Meanwhile, Charles yawned and pulled her pillow over his head in an attempt to get more sleep.

When Mary reached the great room in their small cottage, her mother was just finishing tying the bed to the wall, converting her evening chambers back into a common room. She slept on a folding rope bed that lifted out of the way. This way, snug by the fire, she remained nice and warm. The rest of the room was furnished with a few simple wooden chairs, a round table, a storage chest and a settle bench. Mary and her mother also had a spinning wheel in the corner of the room, which they used to produce yarn.

Her mother turned. "Hello Dear," she greeted.

"Good morning, Mother," answered Mary as she took hold of the bed to help her mother.

"No need to help, Dear. In your condition you should not be straining with this type of labor. I already started the fire in the kitchen and put on the water to boil. You go ahead and work on the morning meal. I'll finish here and work on stoking this fire as well."

Mary's mother, Sarah, had lived with them since November, and she and Mary had dwelt in Charles' home for the past year and a half while Charles had been away at war. Benjamin, Mary's father, had gone with Charles and the army in 1755, but had died of a wound he received at the Battle of Lake George. Living under the same room as your parents, while being married, was a common practice in this generation. It was the least that Charles and Mary could do.

Mary felt flushed when she entered the warmth of the kitchen in the small backroom of the house. She dampened a towel in the copper basin setting on the red cupboard and bathed her face. Feeling refreshed she went on with her business. Today was a special day because of the town meeting, so Mary was preparing more than the usual warmed porridge gruel. She began to fry some salted pork and mixed up the dough for a fresh loaf of bread. Mary placed this loaf in the small bake oven built into the hearth. She then began putting together some dried meat, cheese and cornmeal cakes for a mid-day meal in town.

Charles slid his legs over the bed and rubbed the stiffness from his knees. The wonderful aroma of Mary's cooking had filtered into other rooms, and Charles sniffed eagerly. Slowly he hobbled across the bedchamber to his grandfather's highboy. The hard military service of the past years was beginning to take its toll in the mornings. He pulled clean hose and a shirt out of the highboy and walked back to the foot of the bed where he opened a green painted trunk. He started to pull out clothing and put them on. He began with a pair of blue, woolen breeches and then a red, wool, waistcoat. Charles lifted out a blue coat with red cuffs and lapels and put it on. This was the regimental coat of the Massachusetts-Bay soldiers. Once again, he reached into the trunk and pulled out a red, worn sash with a white stripe running down the middle. To signify his rank as sergeant, he wrapped this sash around his waist.

Several weeks earlier, Charles had been visited by several men who he had served with him in 1755 and 1756. They had discussed the need for well-trained men of honor; men who not only served God and King, but also their brethren soldiers; men who had led others against the French and their heathens; and men who knew the importance of finishing this war in order to protect their families.

Charles was only 24, but he had the experience of such men. He had served alongside his friends and neighbors in 1755 and personally witnessed the hell of war at the Battle of Lake George. Deciding to remain with the army that winter, Charles learned partisan tactics from men such as Putnam, Symes and Rogers. In 1756, he had been given the chance to lead men as a corporal and then was promoted to sergeant. Now, again, Charles had to decide; would he take up the musket and join his comrades to drive God's enemies from North America?

Charles' decision was now made easier, for he would not only have to see to the safety of his family, but he now had a child to protect as well. He must see to his child's future! Charles had reenlisted as a sergeant of Captain Israel Davis' company of Colonel Jonathan Bagley's regiment. His first assignment was to assist in the recruiting of men from his hometown of Amesbury.

After dressing, Charles followed his nose into the kitchen. There he found Mary and Sarah placing the food on the pine, trestle table. The three sat around the table in their banister-back chairs and Charles remarked, "This smells delicious, a meal fit for King George himself!"

"Charles, will you lead us in prayer this morning?" asked Sarah.

They bowed their heads and placed their hands on the table reverently.

"Lord Jehovah, we thank You for this wonderful meal and for this chance to sit here before You this fine, brisk, spring morning. You have not only guided our lives to this point but now bring us new hope with Mary being with child and with the optimism that we march forth soon to attack Your enemies. We ask You, Jehovah, for an easy spring with good rainfall for our crops. Keep all safe who march to do Your work. As we pray in Your name, Amen."

Charles and Sarah began to enjoy the rare morning feast, while Mary only nibbled on a piece of the fresh bread. Charles was concerned.

"Are you not hungry?" he asked.

"It's nothing, only a touch of morning sickness," Mary said meekly. "I have had this feeling for a week now, but you have not noticed as we usually eat meagerly in the morn. I believe it is the salted pork." She put her hand over her mouth.

"Tis normal and healthy for an expecting mother as long as you keep yourself healthy," reassured Sarah.

The three continued their meal and when finished Charles excused himself. He sported his soldier's tricorn hat and took up his sword belt, haversack, canteen and cartridge box from the pegs by the back door. He picked up his Brown Bess musket from the corner as well and left the house to hitch his horse to the wagon.

The wind was brisk but dry. Charles stopped, raised his head to the sky, and closed his eyes. The morning was fresh, and he allowed himself a moment to relax and let the breeze blow over his face. He had been second-guessing his decision to rejoin the army, but truly he must go forth and insure the safety of his family. He walked to the small barn behind the house and hitched the horse to his small wagon. Charles put several heavy lap blankets in the seat, led the horse and wagon out of the barn and up to the back of the house.

Mary and Sarah met him, and Charles helped them into the wagon and covered them with the lap blankets. He then climbed up, snapped the reins, and the horse plodded away from the house. At the end of the lane they turned right onto the Pow Wow River road. The river skirting the left of the road moved swiftly in the morning breeze. The huge, ancient maple trees lining the right of the road waved their limbs with vigor.

A short distance down the road a red saltbox home came into view. On the lane leading from the house was another wagon. It was Charles' parents, Caleb and Margaret, and Charles' younger brother, Enoch. Both families began to wave as they met on the road.

"Good morning!" greeted Caleb.

"Fine morning, father," replied Mary.

"You look well today, dear. Nice to see you Sarah," said Margaret cheerfully to Mary and her mother.

The two wagons then continued down the road heading towards town. Along the route, more families began to appear on the road. About a mile down the road, the wharves and boat building shops lined the Pow Wow River. The third wharf had a ship being rigged, and Charles speculated that she must be about ninety tons. A short distance farther, the Nurses turned their wagons to the north and into the town of Amesbury. From this corner a variety of houses lined both sides of the road, most being modest with small lots. The road became very congested, and toward the top of the knoll rested the town's meetinghouse and congregational church. To its North, lay the village green with stately maples lining the ten acre community-owned parcel. The Nurse families stopped their wagons in front of the village green, and Caleb unhitched their horses. Enoch led them to a shade tree and tied them while the rest of the family made their way into the meetinghouse.

After Charles made sure the Nurse family was seated, he took his place in the rear of the room with other uniformed men. Within minutes the meeting was called to order with a prayer.

A gray haired man dressed in a black suit and wearing a bright, white Geneva collar walked up the aisle and climbed into the raised pulpit in the front of the room. This was Reverend Wells, the town's Congregationalist minister.

"Let us pray," opened the reverend as he closed his eyes. "We praise You for allowing us to gather here in Your house this fine day. We thank You for a mild winter and the fresh spring rains that will increase our bounty to supply our food." The reverend paused and raised his head and arms toward the heavens and continued. "But this is not why we are gathered here, Jehovah; we are here to raise another army to fight Your war against Your enemies, the Papist and their heathens. We have fought in Your battles every generation, and in this war here, in North America, we now pledge to support You once again. Here in Amesbury we have sent You many of our fathers, sons, relatives and friends. We have fought in battle in 1755 and 1756. Now we wish to make this year the final year of this war: marching forth again in Your name and driving Your enemies from this continent!" Reverend Wells put his hands together in reverence and continued, "Lord, we pray for Your success in the ensuing campaign and ask that You bring us back all our loyal volunteers who will join Your army today. They march to fight in Your holy war. Let them be strong! We pray in Your name. Amen."

Looking down upon the people gathered in the room, he made this introduction. "At this time, I welcome the colonel of the third regiment being raised to march next month, our own Colonel Jonathan Bagley."

From the back, a man strode down the aisle at a deliberate gate. Following the colonel was Charles. Charles placed himself beside the deacon's bench. The colonel was nearly six feet tall. He gave a distinguished, statesman-like appearance in his scarlet, gold-laced uniform. Colonel Bagley placed his gold-laced tricorn hat on the deacon's bench and began to pace back and forth in front of the congregation as he talked.

"First off, I would like to thank Reverend Wells for bringing God's blessings to our forming army. Second, I thank you all for coming together and allowing the army's representatives and myself to address you. I have received a commission from our governor to raise a regiment again this year. We will again be marching into New York and attacking the French forts. I have been able to commission part of my officer corps along with some of the corporals and sergeants from the past campaign. As a result, we will have some experienced men leading the regiment. Some of the company commanders are with me today. Captains George and Davis are in the back to talk with you in a moment.

"This may be the last year of this war if we get the support needed. We need to secure the frontier from our enemies before they move to our colony and attack our homes. It is the responsibility of every man to step forward and volunteer for this army, to protect his family and his property against the French. I have here a proclamation that Sergeant Nurse will read to you explaining the terms of service. Sergeant, read the document."

"Sir," answered Charles as he stepped forward, saluted the colonel and began to read. "For the raising of troops in His Majesty's service in the colony of Massachusetts-Bay. If enlisted before March 21 to receive 1 pound, 16 shillings per month, a blanket, coat, soldier's hat and $6 bounty to receive after passing muster. Those who had served in expeditions against Crown Point, Nova Scotia, Kennebeck, had been in bateau service, served as pioneers, served in independent ranging companies under Captain Rogers or employed by the government in defense of the frontiers of the province within the past three years shall also receive $4 bounty by their colonels upon passing muster. No man shall serve more than a 12-month term of service. Also, 5 shillings 8 pence per day from passing muster until they receive the King's allowance; this is above the 2 shillings sterling per week offered by his Lordship." Charles saluted the colonel again and stepped back.

Colonel Bagley continued, "Good-men of Amesbury, I challenge each of you to seek deeply in your soul, to look for the reasons for you to enlist today in this army. You must look beyond the pay. You must look at the safety you will bring to your families by serving to drive out our enemies. I am fully aware of the sacrifices that you will be making by leaving your loved ones at home while you march forth for the summer campaign. But, is this sacrifice worthwhile? Will you be placing your families in such a terrible situation or will it be for the betterment of your families if you come with me and are successful? We can make a difference for the rest of the lives of your families.

"At this time, the good officers of my regiment will step outside and will have a table for you to sign your name on the muster rolls of our regiment. Sergeant Nurse and one of my clerks, John Bush, will assist them. They will be here for an hour if you need time to address the issues with your families before signing. I ask you personally, to step forward at this time and join the Regiment. Help your families, your colony, your King and God."

Bagley picked up his hat. He and Charles walked down the aisle followed out the front doors by Captains George and Davis and clerk Bush.

Outside Charles and Bush took a seat at a log table while the captains stood behind them to answer questions and see that everything remained legal. John and Charles had known each other slightly from 1755 when John came to Fort William Henry that November and stayed through the winter. John was a Negro, a freeman from Shrewsbury. He was a superb engraver and scribe in civilian life. Both Charles and John were clerks in Bay Colony regiments that year.

Men began to line up and approach the table. Levi Whitcomb was one of the first. He had served in 1756 in Bagley's Regiment.

"Where do I sign, Sergeant?"

Charles pointed to the next line in the Regimental Book and directed, "here Levi, on this line if you will."

"I served in '55' and I'm a guessin' it's about time I go after those Frenchmen again," boasted Isaac Martin.

"Then sign the Regimental Book on this line," said Charles.

Looking up from the table, Charles saw Joseph Nichols and Thomas Greenleaf.

"I was wondering if I would see you two today. Didn't get enough last year?" asked Charles.

"We couldn't resist if you're to be our sergeant," joked Thomas.

"That's right. Except the money sounded awful good too," added Joseph.

"Then glad to have you aboard for another campaign. Sign the book here, and we'll make soldiers out of you again," responded Charles.

The officers and the rest of the recruiting party were pleased with the enlistments. Colonel Bagley was also pleased when he commissioned Joseph Greenleaf as an Ensign and re-enlisted Nathaniel Ingersoll as a Lieutenant. After an hour, everyone was dismissed.

The families loaded their carts and wagons and headed for home. Charles and Mary usually talked for a few minutes in bed before falling asleep. This night though, Charles just lay there without saying a word. Mary rolled over and put her arms around Charles.

"What is bothering you?" asked Mary.

"Nothing," answered Charles.

"Is it the idea that you are leaving for the army again next month?" she asked.

"I think I may have made the wrong decision. I must have been selfish. We have a child on the way, and I'm leaving you. How can this be the right choice?" replied Charles.

"Charles, you should not feel bad about your choice. We talked about it and knew then that I was with child. I am proud of your decision to fight the enemy again. You would not be the man I married if you didn't follow your heart. You think of your family and how you can make our future secure. You should think about our child. You need to realize that by marching with this army, you will make a difference. You can make this country, this land a better place for him. You do not need to worry about me; I have your parents and my mother to see to my needs. They will take care of me. I feel safe with the sacrifice that you are keeping the French away from us and securing our colony forever," reassured Mary.

"I guess you are right. It's just hard to live with the idea that I am leaving you, especially at this time. What will you do if I do not come back?" he asked.

"Charles Nurse, I'll hear no such talk. You will come back! Your child and I will be waiting for you! Enough of this, let's go to sleep," said Mary sternly.

"Good night Dear," whispered Charles as he kissed her goodnight.

"Good night, I love you," said Mary.

The next month Charles and Mary spent making preparations for his departure. The farm needed to be readied for the spring, and the house needed some repair. Charles also needed some time with his parents and with Mary. They would be apart for months.

A SOLDIER AGAIN

The day came and the levies from Amesbury, Newbury and the other surrounding towns formed, joining Bagley's Regiment as it marched along its route from northeast Massachusetts south to Boston. Upon reaching Boston, the troops rendezvoused and continued west toward the frontier and the Hudson River. The march was long but not too challenging until reaching the hills in western Massachusetts. Along the way, the soldiers spent nights in barns, taverns and in fields. Marching was from sun up to sun down. After twenty-five days the regiment reached Albany in New York Colony.

For two weeks, the men in Charles' regiment encamped on the Albany Flats just north of the town. Regiments and pieces of them from many colonies, including Massachusetts, continued arriving daily. Stores, equipment and armaments were readied and most troops spent most of their days training and exercising their firelocks. All preparations were being made, and by the first week in June many portions of the army began their march north toward Fort Edward.

The terrain was very familiar to parts of Bagley's Regiment. Those like Charles, who had marched here before, knew what to expect and arrived at Fort Edward in good spirits in just under two weeks.

With the arriving of the army, Fort Edward was a bustling mass of soldiery. Men from the regular regiments of King George, provincials, carpenters and other specialists were training and scouting, as well as preparing the fort, wagons and bateaus for movement north to Lake George. Soldiers ranged from well-disciplined regulars to raw country recruits. The challenge at this point was for the commanders to move the army to Fort William Henry and then to transport them on the lake to attack the French Fort Carillon.

Charles had been busy as a company sergeant leading work parties and working on training his men. One late afternoon he walked south of Fort Edward and found a comfortable spot under a large oak. Here he sat down, laid out his quill and ink, and removed his letter book from his haversack to write a letter to Mary.

My dearest Mary,

I have been busy these past two months and now find time to write you telling that I have made it safe to Fort Edward. I feel ashamed that it has taken me so long to pen this letter for I know how much you are probably worrying.

Our march was uneventful, arriving in Albany in good order. We only dallied there for two weeks, unlike the last campaigns. We then marched north to Fort Edward making good time. This is a much better route than in the past as the road and river crossings have been kept up by the army, unlike the past two years.

Much of our time here is spent working on the fort and preparing boats for movement to Fort William Henry. This fort has much changed from what you would remember. The road leading north, up the Hudson now crosses and progresses up the western shore. Once you reach near the middle of the island, you cross the river and walk over the island to another bridge to the main entrance into the fort. The island is used now to quarter ranger companies, many of the provincial troops in tents, and headquarters for the fort's commander. On the southern end of the island we have also been working on finishing a smallpox hospital. This distemper is beginning to greatly affect the troops of this army. The surgeons want to keep these men away from the others. There is also a large garden planted on the island which men tend daily. This is to supply fresh rations for us.

At the fort, the flagstaff has been placed on the northeastern bastion. In the northwest bastion we have built a new magazine. There are now two officers' barracks on each side of the north gate and just outside this gate we are now working on a large redoubt. The old hospital has been replaced with a large barracks on the west side of the fort. It is 25 feet by 150 feet and two stories tall. It garrisons 100 regulars and has a hospital room within. There is a passageway built though the center of the lower story that leads to the west gate into the fort.

There are several here that have made it tolerable so far. I am doing my utmost to not slip back into the debauchery from the previous campaign. We have some good officers. Colonel Bagley has chosen wisely. Samuel George and John Taplin are again captains in the regiment. We have a new captain, Israel Davis. Last year he served as a lieutenant. His family is one of the oldest in the colony, hailing from Danvers. I have been placed in his company.

I have some men who are veterans, which makes parts of my job easier. Joseph Nichols, Thomas Greenleaf and Gideon Lowell are in my squad. Thomas' cousin, Joseph is also one of our ensigns. There are several new men who are fine soldiers. Some are Jonathan Baily of Rowley, John and Thomas Jones from Ipswich and William Warren, whom I believe you know from Amesbury.

The past weeks since arriving here at Fort Edward have been spent with mundane tasks. I have been on few scouts. Because of our skills, many of our company have been utilized in building and repairing work around the fort. I do look forward to moving north. If this army stagnates here too long, I feel nothing may be accomplished. So far, all are in good spirits.

There are thousands of men stationed here and at Fort William Henry. This year we have many redcoats quartered here as well: more than in the past. Some seem to be decent fellows, but others it is hard to believe are Englishmen like us. Yesterday, our entire garrison was mustered and reviewed by a regular named Major Fletcher. His regiment is the King's 35th of Foot and he is also the commander at the fort. He had the martial law read to us. This law seems too strict to abide, but it is the law and unless our officers and legislatures find a way to have us under our own provincial military laws we must abide by them.

I so hope that you are doing fine. With only two months remaining until you give birth to our child, you must be getting miserable and uncomfortable. I wish so that I could be with you to comfort and hold you and to see to your every need. I have also written to my parents asking mother to check on you and to engage Goody Greenleaf to serve as your midwife. I am sure that between her, your mother, and mine, that you will have all needed for a safe birthing. Remember always, Dear, that I love you and with any luck I will be home early this fall.

Yours Affectionately,
Charles

The next day Major Fletcher marched south to Saratoga with a party of thirty of his regiment, twenty of the 60th regiment and eighty from the Bay Colony. Charles and Captain Davis' company were in this party. The duty of this group was to act as escort for the new commander of the forts, Major General Daniel Webb. They arrived around 4 o'clock in the afternoon, but the general was not yet at Saratoga. Consequently, the escort from Fort Edward waited on him. At 11 o'clock the next morning the General finally arrived at Saratoga. The escort party then marched him to Fort Edward where they arrived late in the afternoon.

On July 1, Charles was working on the new fascine battery. In the afternoon a runner from the rangers came into the fort from the north. The ranger ran from the edge of the woods towards where Charles and his men were working.

"Hold, what's your business!" bellowed Charles at the ranger.

Out of breath the ranger stated, "I'm seak'en reinforcement for Captain Putnam. We've attacked ye enemy at South Bay!"

"Corporal, take him to General Lyman's tent immediately," ordered Charles.

The man was escorted directly to the General's tent. Within minutes the General came out of his quarters and began issuing orders. The drummer posted at his tent began to beat assembly, and the garrison of the fort and encampment on the island began to form. Charles and his work party made their way quickly to their point of formation with the rest of his regiment and poised for whatever was coming next. Within a few moments the officers approached their regiments.

"Sergeants, step forward," ordered Major Miller of Bagley's regiment to his NCOs.

The sergeants, including Charles, marched up to the Major and saluted by recovering their muskets.

"The General has received word that Captain Putnam is in need of reinforcement near Wood Creek where he has attacked a large enemy party. I am looking for two sergeants who will volunteer to join this relief party with twelve men under each," instructed the major.

"Sir," answered Charles. "I volunteer."

"I also volunteer, sir," stated Isaac Martin.

"Very well, gentlemen," said Major Miller with authority. "Get twelve volunteers each from the regiment and prepare for the four-day scout. Draw rations and ammunition for your men from the quartermaster."

Charles was persuasive and got Joseph Nichols, Thomas Greenleaf, Gideon Lowell, Levi Whitcomb, Jonathan Bailey, Abel Blake, Ballard Smith, John Jones, Thomas Jones, John Peirce, Jonathan Rogers, and William Hubbard to volunteer for his party. It took only one hour, and Charles had his men equipped and formed on the fort's parade with almost 300 others. The two parties of Bagley's men were placed in command of Lieutenant Nathaniel Ingersoll from Bagley's Regiment. Charles and his men were given the right flank of the march.

Within minutes the relief column was on the move. The point guards jogged across the open ground heading northeast to the woods about eighty rods away. Following was the main party of the column marching in their tracks north with men extended on their left and right flanks and a like party trailing behind to make sure the enemy could not circle around them and attack. Once reaching the woods the main party of the column followed the old Fort Nicholson's road, the road that lead to the ruins of old Fort Anne and Wood Creek.

Lyman and the relief column moved at a quick march, hoping if Putnam was still engaged he could reach them in time. About three and a half miles down the road the column was halted while the forward scouts made sure there was no enemy lurking at the river crossing at Fort Edward Creek. Once secured, the column resumed its march. On the left, in the distance, they could see the lowlands of the South Bay region and just beyond, the mountains. To the right, the forest was flat with intermixed swamp.

As they progressed, the lush green canopy of the climax forest kept the direct sun from beating down upon the troops. The humidity was not extreme this day and the men continued in good order.

Just as the sun began to drop slightly, the column was again stopped. Charles was at the head of the right flank party and could see that they were just nearing the old field that surrounded the old fort. To his right, Charles could see East Creek, a tributary of Wood Creek, which now skirted the road.

Orders were given, and Charles and his men scouted to the east of the old fort's clearing. They advanced into the woods to the east and crossed the creek. As soon as they crossed the creek, they spread out, leaving twenty-feet between each man, and slowly marched farther east and then turned northeast. After about one half hour Charles called a halt and led his men into the clearing toward the old fort. As they approached the clearing, they could see men from the main column that had been posted as guards just inside the woods.

The clearing was not large, approximately twenty rods. To the south was the road they had just passed; to the east was East Creek, to the west ran Forks Creek, and to the north was Wood Creek. Roughly in the center of the forest opening stood the remnants of an old stockade that measured nearly four rods. A two-story blockhouse stood inside the stockade. Once the men saw to their needs, darkness was approaching and General Lyman saw it fitting for the ruins to service as this night's quarters for his men. Security was organized for the night while several scouts were sent north, one on the west side of Wood Creek, one along the east. The others attempted to get what sleep they could.

The next morning, scouting parties were sent in different directions while a main detachment was held at the base camp to reinforce them if they found the enemy. Charles was ordered to take his men to the west.

"I want total silence on the march. I'll take point, Thomas take the rear guard, Blake take our left and Smith you have our right. The rest keep spread apart so if the enemy shoots, it will not take out more than one of you with one ball. Let's march," ordered

Charles. The men entered the woods and spread out taking up their assigned positions.

Within an hour something had been found. Abel Blake called a halt. Closest to Charles was Jon Bailey.

"Bailey, keep your eyes on our front," whispered Charles. Charles snapped his fingers and pointed to three men who came over to him.

"Hubbard, Jones, Nichols with me," ordered Charles as the four sprinted toward Blake's position.

Charles knelt down beside Bailey.

"I've found one of Putnam's men," whispered Bailey as he pointed to a boulder.

"Charles walked over and looked behind it. John Jones had followed Charles over to the rock. Jones took one look at the corpse and vomited.

Charles stared at the corpse for a moment. Finally, he was able to recognize the person, despite the grotesque mutilations. It was one of Putnam's Mohegans, Henry Shuntup. He was covered in dried blood. His lips had been cut off down to his chin and up to his nose and his jaw was laid bare. His scalp was taken off and his breast was cut open like a butchered cow with a bullet bag in place of his heart. His left hand was still clenched around his gall from the pain. His fingernails had all been pulled off for torture. Still in his bowels stuck a tomahawk, and a spear stuck through him as well. The little finger and toe from his left hand and foot were missing, strange trophies along with the scalp.

"Nichols, get a couple of men and bury him. There won't be enough for us to carry back to the fort."

"Eye, Sergeant," replied Joseph.

Few other signs were found of the enemy or Putnam's party. The relief column continued to scout the areas around Wood Creek for the next day and a half, finding little more than tracks and a site where the enemy was believed to have stayed the night. The afternoon of the fourth day out, Lyman and his column marched back to Fort Edward.

Several weeks passed, and Charles was preparing to march north to Fort William Henry. He found a comfortable place on the west side of the Hudson, still within the guard perimeter, and sat down to pen a note to his parents and Mary.

Dear Mother and Father,
Work here at Fort Edward has been quite steady. We have progressed quite well on the fortifications and have been also employed in a few scouts along with some ranger companies, escort duty between here and Saratoga, and repaired wagons and carts for the transport of any boats that are brought up.

We have been growing worried that the enemy may be heading south to attack either Fort William Henry or here at Fort Edward before we move north to attack them. The natives and some of the scouts have been coming in with prisoners, both French and Indian. Most of them that we get to talk tell that a large force is moving south against us. Many of us believe this to be true. There have been several large enemy parties of natives who have attacked us, one venturing as far south as here at Fort Edward.

About a week ago, I was in camp on the island working on a hospital roof when there was firing in the distance, east of the fort. I knew there was a wood cutting party posted in that direction. Almost immediately, many of the provincials rushed from camp without orders to lend assistance. This created such confusion. Shortly after, the rangers who were to be the first out if attacked, ran from the island around the front of the fort and headed east. The swarm of men pouring from the fort and island put the enemy to flight. Luckily, only the rangers followed the enemy, but could not overtake them. There were few left to defend the fort or island stemming from the confusion. When the casualties were brought in, the garrison was alarmed and many were stricken with terror. The enemy had not attacked with muskets but with bow and arrows. We had never seen such a method of fighting, and rumors spread that the attackers were from the far west, more heathens brought down to invest us like a swarm of locus.

We also have just received word that a large scout of some 350 of the Jersey Blues and Yorkers ventured up Lake George under command of Colonel Parker from New Jersey. They were to destroy an enemy sawmill. Word is that they anchored in the lake at night, and at the break of dawn three of Parker's boats fell into an ambush and surrendered. Shortly after three more boats also fell into the same ambush, all without firing a shot. Then Parker and the other sixteen boats advanced toward the enemy when a huge party of enemy Indians fired on them from shore, which forced his flotilla to fall back. The Indians were quick to respond and jumped in their swift canoes overtaking Parker's men, sinking some of their boats and capturing all but two boats that made an escape. The heathens then jumped in the water and seized the boats turning them over from below. They began spearing many of the soldiers like fish and drowning many others! It was reckoned 200 were captive. Two other boats, including one with Parker, escaped this horror.

The Indians looted the boats, cargo and packs of the soldiers, found rum and guzzled the liquor. This is believed to have caused the Indians to become extremely cruel. They took three prisoners, put them in pots over a fire and cooked them and devoured their bodies. Many of the others were butchered, mutilated and left to rot. The speculation is that 100 men escaped, 100 were killed and 150 remain prisoners, taken north to the enemy forts.

With these atrocities taken together with the many stories that come in from the scouts, the garrison here is becoming jumpy. Also, many are beginning to disobey orders, and the harsh redcoat justice is beginning to rear its ugly head. Yesterday a soldier of the 60th regiment was shot by a firing squad for desertion. Today, a man from the regulars was tied to a gun carriage in the fort and was beaten! It was cruel punishment. The drummer flogged him repeatedly, laying his back open like a gutted fish. The man winced, eventually began to cry out and then lost consciousness. The officer ordered the drummer to continue flogging. Blood ran so thick that it began to ooze from the bottom of the soldier's breeches. An awful day!

I have received only a few letters from you or Mary but believe that it is because of the irregular transport of communications. I take it Mary and the baby are doing fine and that she will be delivering shortly. I do wish that I could be there and pray there are no complications. I intend to also write her today for I have just received orders to move up to Fort William Henry with several other skilled boat builders from our regiment.

I will write you again shortly. Until then I remain your loving son.
Charles

THE SIEGE

The next morning the sun showed bright as Charles crawled from his 'oznaburg tabernacle,' as they called their tents. Joseph had been up earlier and boiled some Indian meal. Charles walked to the mess fire, dipped out a full mug of the gruel, and sat quietly eating his breakfast. Others of his mess did the same and in no time men from the Bay-Colony began striking tents and loading them into wagons for the march to Fort William Henry.

The detachment of ship's carpenters from Bagley's Regiment, of which Charles was part, was to be under the command of Lieutenant Joel Bradford and Ensign Joseph Greenleaf. Charles was the Sergeant and John Peirce was the Corporal. The detachment was also made up of Jonathan Bailey, Abel Blake, John Bush, Thomas Greenleaf, William Hubbard, John Jones, Thomas Jones, Jonathan Rogers, Ballard Smith and William Warren.

At approximately 10 o'clock in the morning, the reinforcements for Fort William Henry had formed. The command of the march was under Lieutenant Colonel Young of the Royal American Regiment. As the column was forming Charles could see Colonel Young receiving his final orders from General Webb. They exchanged salutes, and Colonel Young mounted his horse and rode to the head of the column.

"Captain Faesch, advance the column with full guards," ordered Young.

Faesch saluted the colonel and gave the proper orders placing guards in the advance, rear and both flanks. Rudolphus Faesch was a Swiss officer who had served in the French army. On the march, he had 100 soldiers of the 60th Regiment of Foot under his command. Captain Charles Cruikshanks had 100 men of the Independent Regiment based in New York under his command. Colonel Joseph Frye of Massachusetts had 823 men of his colony, including the attached ship's carpenters. The captains from Massachusetts under Frye's command were Arbuthnot, Ball, Burk, Cheevers, Indicott, Saltonstall, Tapley, Thaxter, and Waldo. They took with them six whaleboats on carts.

The reinforcement column marched along the road between the two forts, progressing nicely until close to half way to Fort William Henry. At this point, one of the carts collapsed. The whaleboat was loaded on top of one of the others and they continued. The problems began to escalate as a wheel on one of the other carts broke. An attempt was made to repair the wheel and they continued. By the time the column made it to Half Way Brook, all five of the remaining carts were in such disrepair that a decision was made to leave the carts and whaleboats there and to return later for them with different carts.

Dusk was just setting in as the column entered the clearing at Lake George. To Charles, the surroundings looked much as they had the previous year. They marched directly to the fort where Lieutenant Colonel Young received orders from the commandant to quarter part of the 35th Regiment, the Independent Company and the Massachusetts troops in the retrenched camp. The 60th and the rest of the 35th were to be placed in the fort, which was commanded by Captain Ormsley of the 35th Regiment.

The retrenched camp was the fortified area west of the fort, the other side of the marshy area. This camp was now roughly 200 yards wide, by 400 long. In the center, stood an entrenchment made of log, about 50 yards square with two cannon emplacements. By the time the provincials marched into the retrenchment, the sun was falling and only a few tents were set up for necessity.

The reinforcements now brought the entire garrison to nearly 2,200 men. Lt. Colonel James Monro commanded them all from his tents in the retrenched camp. He was a graying Scotsman, somewhat short in stature but made up for his height in stamina and courage. Before reinforcements arrived, Monro had in his garrison part of the 35th Regiment of Foot, a detachment of Royal Artillery under Captain Thomas Ord, provincials from New Hampshire commanded by Colonel Gough, Yorkers under command of Captain Ogden, and Jersey Blues under command of Colonel John Parker. A detachment of Rogers' Rangers commanded by Lieutenant Johnson, some artificers from Massachusetts under Captain Ingersoll, some sailors commanded by officers of the 35th Regiment, and several engineers were also under Colonel Monro's command.

The reinforcements found spots within the retrenched camp for their gear and began to cook their evening meal. Charles and his fellow ship's carpenters filled a mess kettle with rice, water, beef and peas and put it on a mess fire. While it was cooking, the men saw to where they would put their bedrolls for the evening and looked out over the stockade at the last glimpse of the setting sun. It didn't take long and the meal was cooked and the men, hungry from their march, devoured the mess kettle's contents.

Charles and Thomas had just finished and saw several military acquaintances walk by.

"Jon Carver," said Charles.

Carver turned and saw Charles. "Nurse, I see you made it back to Lake George again," greeted Carver. "Thomas, good to see you too."

The other man had his back turned away from Charles and Thomas but turned when the conversation began.

"Charles, I thought I'd see you up here at William Henry," said John Bush.

"Sooner or later I end up here. Glad to see you Bush," offered Charles.

"I finished that powder horn for you, Charles," stated Bush. "Come over to our camp, and I'll get it for you."

The four walked over to the south side of the retrenchment to the tents of the Massachusetts troops. John pulled his knapsack from his tent, pulled out a piece of fabric, unwrapped a powder horn and handed it to Charles.

Charles' smile grew large as he examined it. John had engraved a map of the Hudson River and Lake George and pinpointed Fort Edward, Fort William Henry and some of the small outposts also in the area.

"Superb job, John. It looks wonderful."

Bush had started to engrave powder horns for soldiers for extra money this spring, a natural outcrop of his metal engraving in civilian life.

Charles reached in his coat pocket and pulled out a leather wallet. Carefully he counted out the cost of Bush's labor and paid him what he owed.

"Have you seen the lake since arriving?" asked Bush.

"Not yet. I'd like to see it again," answered Thomas.

The four men left the stockade of the retrenchment and walked down to the docks. Several guards stood on the docks searching the water in case of an enemy sighting. Off in the distance along the northwest shore of the bay there were several flashes.

"Did you see that?" asked Charles.

"That's probably the scouting party. One is usually sent out twice a day to reconnoiter along the lake up to the narrows. I saw five whaleboats head out about three hours ago, just about when you were marching in," said Bush assuredly.

"Things, I guess, haven't changed much around here. That's been the standard practice since 1755. I'll wager it was rangers too, wasn't it?" questioned Charles.

"Sure was," stated Carver. "They are commanded here by Lieutenant Noah Johnson. I don't know if you had heard, but Robert Rogers' brother, Richard, died of the pox."

"No, I hadn't heard that; what a shame; a damned good ranger he was," replied Charles with a sad tone.

The four men didn't tarry much longer. It had been a long day's march and Charles and Thomas needed to get some sleep.

A few hours before daybreak, Charles woke suddenly. He must have been aroused by the noise of men stirring. He put on his shoes, regimental coat and hat and walked to the northeast edge of the log wall. He could see several dozen men down by the water and twice as many by the docks in front of the fort. He peered out into the bay and then scanned the shorelines. At the far west end of the bay he could see three large fires. Then he saw the movement of nearly fifty men running from the western woods to the fort. This was the scouting party from the previous evening. Charles speculated that the French might be paying them a visit. Now Charles could no longer sleep so he kindled the mess fire and made some tea.

DAY ONE ❧ *Cut off* ❧

Just as the sun was rising, the drums in the fort began beating. Immediately, the entire garrison of the fort and retrenched camp sprinted to their battle stations. Charles and his men were directed to the southeastern part of the wall with the other Massachusetts soldiers. They formed with one rank standing on the firing platform, muskets pointed outward, and another rank behind. Charles was on the platform at the right of his men. They were poised for battle. Charles' eyes scanned the woods line some eighty rods away.

Suddenly, the cannons on the northwest and northeast bastions of the fort erupted, sending shots over the lake. Charles and most of the soldiers turned their attention to the water. Coming across the horizon toward the entrance to the bay was an enemy flotilla of boats, bateaux and Indian canoes. Puffs of smoke were seen from several French cannon muzzles on floating barges. In about half a minute their explosions were heard. The British cannon shells splashed as they fell short while the French artillery rounds had the same result. Seeing the urgency, Colonel Monro ordered the two 32 pound siege guns fired the warning to Fort Edward that Fort William Henry was under attack. Moments later, a call went out up and down the line that messengers were going out and not to fire on them. Two of Lieutenant Johnson's rangers sprinted from the retrenched camp down the road toward Fort Edward. They carried the following dispatch to General Webb.

Sir,

This is to acquaint you that the enemy is in sight upon the lake, and we know that they have cannon. They cut off our two boats between two and three this morning that were towards our first island. As yet we know nothing of their numbers.
I am your Obedient Servant,
Geo. Monro, Lt. Col. to 35th Regiment

It was not long and the enemy began popping up from all along the tree line, skulking, spying and surrounding the retrenched camp and fort. The enemy's native allies were encircling the British. Part of the Indians made their way to a small stockade where the oxen and horses that had come up from Fort Edward the previous day were corralled. With yells and whoops they released the animals, chasing many of them down and leading them into the woods.

Colonel Monro was greatly disturbed by the sight of a group of natives beginning to form on the road toward Fort Edward. Knowing the prudence in securing his communication lines with General Webb, he quickly dispatched 100 Massachusetts men under Captain Saltonstall. The men were hastily formed and the officers given orders. Charles, Joseph, Thomas, Abel Blake and Ballard Smith were in this detachment.

"Captains Arbuthnott and Ingersoll take your Massachusetts men with part of the 35th Regiment and reinforce the fort. Captain Saltonstall, at the quick march, get your men into that road and overpower any enemy you find. I must have possession of that road!" yelled Monro.

Saltonstall stepped quickly to the front of the detachment, drew his sword and bellowed, "Follow me men, at the quick march, MARCH!"

The Massachusetts men began a rapid march out the gate of the log retrenchment and down the road leading to the woods. Just about twenty rods away from the wood's edge Saltonstall ordered Ensign Williams and the first twenty-five men forward at the double quick. Williams and his men rushed forward sprinting the last part of the clearing. Shortly behind them came Saltonstall and the remainder of the detachment.

Saltonstall and his men could see Williams and his detachment still moving quickly as they reached the intersection of the road and the woods. Simultaneously, the trees erupted with smoke, flames and musket balls from in front and along the flanks of Williams' unit striking half of them dead instantly. The rest of Williams' men grabbed whom they could and turned about running back toward camp.

Saltonstall formed a third of his men on the road as an anchor, allowed the others to take cover in the trees on both flanks of the road and lay down covering fire. Within minutes the remnants of Williams' men were safe behind Saltonstall, and savages began to pour out into the road, bounding from tree to tree in the forest like a huge heard of deer. Saltonstall, seeing the overwhelming numbers, pulled his men back and began a firing retreat back toward the log retrenchment.

Seeing the retreat of the Massachusetts men, Colonel Monro ordered supporting fire from the two bronze 6-pounders on the entrenchment. Grape shot spewed from the bronze 12-pounder on the wall facing the road. This kept the natives from breaching the clearing. Once the cannons began their supporting fire, Saltonstall and his Massachusetts men made quick time of returning behind the safety of the retrenchment.

Once the Massachusetts men were inside the retrenchment, the enemy quickly encircled the fort and entrenched camp, and began a continual small arms fire. Colonel Monro ordered return fire from the soldiers and from the cannons loaded with grape shot. This had good effect on the enemy Indians, keeping them from assaulting the British works.

At 11 o'clock in the morning, French drums began to beat. A party of the enemy marched from the west side of the lake toward the fort carrying a red flag, a flag of truce. All firing was halted. As the enemy approached the British could see several drummers, a flag bearer, an officer and a dozen French grenadiers. They stopped five rods from the fort walls. Captain Ormsby marched out of the fort with a white flag, three drummers and a dozen grenadiers. He marched to the French detachment, blindfolded the French officer, and Ormsby and part of his detachment led the Frenchman to the retrenched camp, leaving the rest of his party with the French detachment.

Upon reaching the tent of Colonel Monro, the blindfold was taken off the French officer.

The Frenchman removed his tricorn hat and doffed it in a salute. Colonel Monro raised his hand placing it against the front of his hat, returning the salute. The French officer stated in broken English. "Sir, I am Monsieur Funtbrune. The Marquee de Montcalm has sent me. Here is a letter from the general."

Monro took the letter from Funtbrune and read it.

Sir,

I have this morning invested your place with a numerous Army, a superior artillery and all the savages from the higher parts of the country, the cruelty of which a detachment of your garrison have lately too much experienced. I am obliged in humanity to desire you to surrender your fort. I have it yet in my power to restrain the savages, and oblige them to observe a capitulation as hitherto, none of them have been killed, which will not be in my power in other circumstances and your insisting on defending your fort can only retard the loss of it a few days, and must of necessity expose an unlucky garrison, who can receive no succors, considering the precautions I have taken, I demand a decisive answer immediately for which purpose I have sent you the

Monsieur Funtbrune, one of my aid de camps. You may credit what he will inform you as from me.
I am with Respect,
Your most humble Servant,
Montcalm

Colonel Monro was quite taken aback at the audacity of the French general asking for the surrender of Fort William Henry and his entire garrison. Monro quickly dictated to a scribe the following response.

Sir,

The only answer I can give to your letter is that I am determined to defend the Fort to the last, and I believe it is the resolution, of every man under my command, I am with the greatest regard.
Your most humble Servant,
Geo. Monro, Lt. Col. To 35th Regiment

As soon as Monsieur Funtbrune received Monro's return message he was blindfolded once more and led back to his guards outside of the fort. Both parties then returned to their camps and shortly after a continual firing commenced from Indian and French muskets. Monro then ordered return fire from muskets from the entrenched camp and fort's cannons. This fire continued all day.

Toward nightfall Colonel Monro thought it prudent to send off a runner with another communication to General Webb at Fort Edward.

Sir,
This place was so suddenly surrounded by the enemy that there was no sending off an express. Captain Ogden of the New York detachment has three letters of mine to you, which he could not send off hitherto, I hope this one I now write will be sent off tonight. General Montcalm sent his aid de camp with a letter to me to surrender the Fort and camp. My answer, 'that we were determined to defend both the Fort and the Camp to the last,' they have not yet erected their batteries, but the Indians have been firing upon us from the woods all day. Captain Cunningham of the 35th Regiment is wounded in the arm, and a Corporal of the same regiment has

had his arm cut off, and a few men wounded. I forgot to tell you General Montcalm says in his letter, 'he has a numerous army and superior artillery to ours,' I make no doubt of this.
I am your Obedient Servant,
Geo. Monro, Lt. Col. to 35th Regiment

DAY TWO ~ Another Failed Attempt

It became apparent that the enemy was digging entrenchments in order to place their artillery. From the northwest bastion of Fort William Henry the French had success in landing their artillery. The natives, again, were peppering the fort and retrenched camp with musket fire. Seeing the enemy attempting to bring up supplies to within 100 to 125 rods of the British fortifications, Colonel Monro ordered an annoyance with the firing of mortars and howitzers. This did retard the enemy's work.

Cannonading continued all morning. Problems began to appear with the guns. One of the great mortars burst and had to be replaced by a howitzer. Only minor injuries occurred in this explosion. Around ten o'clock in the morning, one of the barrels of the fort's eighteen pounders split. Lieutenant Collins of the Royal Artillery and Lieutenant Williamson, an engineer, who were in charge of the British artillery understood the stress being placed on the iron guns, so they gave orders that the iron guns were to be cooled after every twelfth round.

Around noon, a man sprinted across the open area of the retrenched camp from the redoubt nearest the lake to the entrenched area where Colonel Monro's command tent stood.

"Sir," stated the man as he saluted. "It looks like the French Indians are trying to cut off access to the lake."

"Colonel Frye," ordered Monro, "get one hundred of your Massachusetts men to attack and dislodge the Natives who are trying to get between us and the water."

Frye immediately sent a message to Captain Waldo, to march with the picket guards of the Massachusetts Regiment and any volunteers that could move as quickly and perform Colonel Monro's orders. Charles and Lieutenant Bradford, Thomas, John Peirce and Ballard Smith quickly joined the detachment. They hustled out the retrenchment gate, moving quickly into the woods under the covering fire of the cannons.

As soon as they hit the tree line they could see a force of natives charging at them. The two groups of warriors collided with great force as bayonets, axes and knives flashed, slashed at each other. Seeing that over half of the Massachusetts men were keeping the Indians at bay, Captain Waldo drew his sword and led a charge with the remaining men through the trees toward the north and the lake. The men, including Charles and his detachment, pushed forward continually receiving flanking fire from other Indians. About six rods from the lake there was a huge volley from a hidden Indian force on the eastern flank, which dropped about one half of the Waldo's force in its tracks. Waldo himself was shot through the body and Lieutenant Bradford and Smith, and Pierce took bullets in the leg and head. Every man that could, returned fire, and most carried or helped the wounded back toward the initial engagement. Once there, two men were sent with a message for the colonel to concentrate their artillery fire 100 yards into the woods, giving covering fire to the men retreating back across the field.

With great thunderous explosions the remaining mortar and howitzers began to place exploding bombs in the woods over the heads of the natives who had the Massachusetts men pinned down. Seizing the moment, the Massachusetts men from Waldo's attack forces, moved as quickly as possible back into the retrenched camp. The wounded men were treated. Waldo was given little hopes of recovery. The rest of the men were either released or were to be released from the surgeon's care the following day.

Now it was believed that the Indians controlled the waterway of communications as well as land. The rest of the day the French continued their trench work and the Indians kept up their small arms fire. Toward nightfall, Colonel Monro wrote once more to General Webb.

Sir,
I must report today that I believe that the enemy has possession of all my communication with you both by land and water. Captain Waldo led a force today to drive the enemy Indians from keeping us from the lake. He was unsuccessful and I fear is dying. He has

received what the surgeons are saying is a mortal wound through the body.

I have not yet received any word from you, and expect a message or reinforcements at any time. If this is not the case, I request again you march the entire army at once to this fort for our relief. At this time the enemy is keeping their regulars out of range and is working on artillery trenching and gun emplacements. I am not expecting the enemy to open fire with their artillery for another day. The natives today have continually harassed us both here in the retrenched camp and the fort with small arms fire. I have given orders for the roofs to be pulled from the barracks, should the enemy open fire with incendiary shot.

Our spirits are high that you are marching with reinforcement as I write. So far this evening, all is quiet. I have given orders that fires are to be burned all night to insure that the Indians do not attempt an attack in the darkness.

I am your Obedient Servant,
Geo. Monro, Lt. Col. to 35th Regiment

DAY THREE ↜ Artillery Dual ↝

Early this day, Charles and most of the army were awoken when the French opened fire with their artillery. They began with their thirteen-inch mortars. These rained devastation on the fort and retrenched camp, showering shrapnel everywhere from fused mortar bombs. Those who were not busied in the fort or retrenchment working the British cannons kept their heads down and sought what cover that was available. The bombardment brought shattering noise to the already tense situation. One after the other the French fired their nine pieces of artillery: the largest firing eighteen-pound solid shots. Several shots were found that had British broad arrows on them, signifying them as King's issued. Many speculated that they were captured from Oswego or General Braddock's defeat.

The early morning was also busied with the moving of ample supplies and provisions from the fort to the retrenched camp. This was done in case a separation occurred between the two camps.

Later in the morning, one of the enemy's solid shot hit the pulley on the flagpole in the northeast bastion of the fort sending the

British flag fluttering. Triumphant cheers rose from the French shouting, "vivre roi,' 'vivre roi,' vivre roi!"(Long live the King)

Two carpenters immediately grabbed the flag and ran it back up the pole. Just as it reached the top, another enemy shell tore off one of the soldiers' heads sending blood spurting from his neck. It took nearly ten seconds for his body to fall, which sent terror into all who witnessed it.

The enemy artillery caused other deaths and wounds this day. One Massachusetts soldier had his leg ripped off by an eighteen-pound French shell while he stood guard at Colonel Frye's tent. The ball was so close to getting the Colonel that it bored through a corner of the canvas.

The British continued return artillery barrages the rest of the day. Taking its toll from the constant firing, one of their 18-pounders and a twelve-pounder burst. One of the six pounders was also ruined from a shot from the enemy guns.

In the afternoon two rangers came sprinting in the retrenched camp.

One man, when reaching the wall, yelled out, "I have an urgent message for Colonel Monro from General Webb!"

"This way," ordered the sergeant of the guard.

The ranger was escorted directly to the colonel's tent.

"Speak man, what is your message," said Monro sharply.

Huffing and puffing the rangers began.

"We have Indians. Colonel Johnson arrived this morning at the fort. He is expecting to march today."

"What about Webb and his garrison? Have they also been attacked? Is he sending a relief column?" questioned Monro.

"I was told to make haste and get the message to you that Johnson had just arrived, but nothing was mentioned of a relief column. The fort has not been attacked. The general has not received much word from you. He knows you are under attack and that is about all. We knew that three days ago when we heard your signal guns. Everyone is very anxious, but I never saw nor heard about any relief."

"Get this man some rum," said Monro.

Suddenly there was a large explosion from the fort. The officers in Monro's tent jumped up and left the tent to see what had made the noise. There was much smoke coming from the northwest bastion and men running about, which looked like they were attempting to assist wounded soldiers. A runner came from the fort bringing a message that the thirty-two-pounder on that bastion had burst. It had damaged the bastion and wounded most of the men attending the gun.

"Damn! Lieutenant Collins, have two of the remaining 12 pounders moved from the entrenched camp to the fort. I must keep a bombardment from those bastions. It's the only way to slow the enemy. Webb must get us more guns and reinforcements," directed Monro.

At evening, Colonel Monro sat down and composed another letter to General Webb.

Sir,
Today the enemy has opened their first battery of nine pieces. They have caused considerable damage to soldiers by exploding bombs from their thirteen-inch mortar. I have had poor luck with some of my artillery, losing a thirty-two, a twenty-four, and an eighteen-pounder, all bursting. I also lost a twelve pounder from an enemy shell.

Much of my men are keeping up good spirits but I know not how long that will be. Mr. Waldo has died this morning form his wounds yesterday.

I received the messenger from you this afternoon, but could not make out what you were hoping to tell me. All he could communicate was that Colonel Johnson has arrived at Fort Edward with a reinforcement of Natives.

I intend on a continuing cannonading on the enemy trenches roughly every fifteen minutes, lasting all night.

I plead with you, sir, for reinforcement here at my fort. I must ask that you march immediately, if you have not already done so, with more cannon and men to increase my garrison. I can hold off the enemy for quite a time being, but my resources will be greatly strained if relief is not received.
I am your Obedient Servant,
Geo. Monro, Lt. Col. to 35th Regiment

DAY FOUR ❧ Intercepted Letter ❧

At six o'clock in the morning, the French opened up a second battery. This right battery consisted of two eighteen-pounders, five twelve-pounders, one eight-pounder, and two seven-inch howitzers and a six-inch mortar. It appeared that the French had several hundred soldiers digging in a third trench as well.

Of course, the British answered with kindness and returned bombardment. At nine o'clock, the French fired volleys from both their batteries. Shortly, a red flag appeared from the forward trench and an officer, drummer and fifteen French grenadiers began marching toward the fort with the red flag of truce. At the edge of the fort's garden, British guards halted the enemy. Two English officers, a drummer and fifteen grenadiers of the 35th Regiment marched out from the fort and presented themselves to the enemy party.

"What is your business?" questioned Lieutenant Adam Williamson, one of the British officers.

In broken English, one of the French officers answered, "Monsiuar, je mappelle, Louis Antonine de Bougainville, aid de camp of General Marquis de Montcalm, with a message for your commander."

"I must blindfold you and lead you to him," answered Williamson. "I will, of course, leave Lieutenant Hamilton with your soldiers to ensure your safe conduct."

"Merci," replied Bougainville.

The Frenchman was then blindfolded, led to the fort and thence to the retrenched camp. The blindfold then was removed and Lt. Williamson presented him to Colonel Monro.

"This is Louis Antonine de Bougainville."

"Je mappelle, Colonel George Monro," offered Monro. "What message do you have for me?"

"Sir, my general, Marquis do Montcalm, has honored me to bring you these letters," stated Bougainville as he handed a letter to the colonel. The colonel sat and read the letters.

Montcalm was very gracious in his writings, instructing the colonel that no harm was meant to come to him directly, and that his intention was to offer him a chance to surrender his fort and his garrison. The colonel then opened the other enclosed letter and read it.

Sir,
I am directed by General Webb to acknowledge the receipt of two of your letters. One bearing date about nine o'clock yesterday morning, and the other about six o'clock in the evening, by two rangers, which are the only men that have got in here except two yesterday morning.

The colonel looked up at the French officer for a moment in astonishment, and then continued his reading.

Your first, acquainting him of the enemy's being in sight, he has ordered me to acquaint you that he does not think it prudent (as you know his strength at this place) to attempt a junction or to assist you until reinforced by the militia of the colonies for the immediate march of which repeated expresses have been sent. One of our scouts brought in a Canadian prisoner last night from the investing party, which is very large, and has possessed all the grounds five miles on this side of Fort W.H. The number of the enemy is very considerable, the prisoner says 11,000, and they have a large train of artillery with mortars and were to open their batteries this day.

The colonel again looked up. He did not say anything for a moment. Then he ordered one of his aid de camps to get Bougainville some wine. Visibly moved, he went back to his reading.

The General thought proper to give you this intelligence that in case he should be so unfortunate as from the delays of the militia not to have it in his power to give you timely assistance, you might be able to make the terms left in your power. The bearer is sergeant of the Connecticut forces, and if he is happy enough to get in, will bring advices from you. We keep continual scouts going to endeavor to get in, and bring intelligence from you.
I am, sir, Your most obedient and humble servant,
George Bartman
Aid de Camp

Monro laid the letters aside but did not speak.

"Je vous accorde ls honneurs de querre (I offer you the honors of war)," spoke Bougainville.

Monro paused and then replied to him in French, "Ce pays estan Roi Georges d'Angleterre (These are King George's lands)! You may tell your general that I need no terms, and I thank him for the pleasures in dealing with such an honorable and generous enemy. We intend to stay behind these walls and defend the King's property. Lieutenant, return the Frenchman."

Bougainville was blindfolded once more and marched back to his escort. The officers were exchanged, and both parties returned to their respective camps.

Almost the second the British grenadiers entered the fort's gates, the enemy cannons opened fire again. Also, while the parley was going on, some of the enemy Indians, Canadians and French regulars had worked their way around to the rear of the fort. Captain Tapley of Massachusetts had been posted there with eighty men and was hidden behind a log redoubt. Seeing the enemy approaching Tapley's men in much greater numbers, Captain Saltonstal of Massachusetts and Captain Crookshanks and part of his Independents, 200 men, were dispatched to assist. These men and Tapley's, being greatly outnumbered, slowed the enemy and engaged for nearly three hours. The enemy was reinforced from hidden men in the woods, forcing Tapley, Saltonstal and Crookshanks' forces to fall back to the camp. Over fifty men were killed and quite a few wounded, but they kept **the enemy from** breaching the retrenched camp's lines.

At sundown Monro attempted to send another letter to General Webb.

Sir,

The Fort & Camp still hold out in hopes of a speedy relief from you, which we hourly expect; and if that does not happen, we must fall into the hands of our enemies.

I, today, had an officer of the enemy come into our camp under a flag of truce. He delivered unto me two letters: one from the Marquis de Montcalm offering me terms for the surrender of my fort and its garrison; the other letter was yours of the fourth, in which

you had encouraged me to sue for terms. The enemy had intercepted the Connecticut man who was the currier. Your letter has greatly helped the enemy. In regards to the numbers of the enemy that you mention, everyone here is of the opinion that they are greatly magnified; if they really had those numbers, they might have demolished us at once, without loss of time.

The French know that you at this time do not intend on reinforcing our garrison here at Fort William Henry. I urge you to gain as many militias as possible and march here to our relief. I believe we can withstand several more days of French shelling as long as they cannot make it much nearer to the fort walls.

My garrison, today, is becoming much forlorn. They have endured days of constant bombardment and have been deprived of sleep. The pox and other camp distempers are spreading through my garrison. The regimental surgeons have made a hospital of sorts in the casements of the fort. Our supplies are adequate but we have lost more cannons today. One of our twelve-pounders and one of our six-pounders have burst. A French howitzer shell hit and exploded one of the ammunition boxes on the northwest bastion, killing sixteen of our men and wounding several others. It was so severe that one of the Massachusetts officer's bodies on that bastion has not been found. A piece of his coat is all that has been recovered.

At approximately noon today, Captain Ormsby of the 35th was severely wounded by a bursting mortar round, which fell into the barracks of the fort. I placed Captain William Arbuthnot of Massachusetts in charge of the fort. He felt there were others more worthy and wished for another officer to be placed in charge of the fort, and he would gladly serve under him. Lieutenant Giles Collins of the Royal Artillery now commands the fort.

I posted evening orders to the garrison that if any person proves cowardly or offers to advise giving up the fort that he should be immediately hanged over the walls of the fort.

I am expecting the bombardment will continue all night.
I am your Obedient Servant,
Geo. Monro, Lt. Col. to 35th Regiment

DAY FIVE ❧ *Will it hold* ❧

At daybreak the officers from the fort's bastions could see through their field glasses that the French had made great progress digging the night before. Now the enemy had a trench nearly fifty rods down a hill and to the swamp, where they built a wet ditch to the edge of the fort's garden. The wet ditch appeared to be filled with fascines on which they laid a road with gabions and parapets to protect its sides. Then with their ingenuity, they covered the ditch with planking.

The British cannons and some muskets were aimed at a new French battery off this new trench as the enemy was attempting to finish it in open daylight. Despite the British cannonading, French work continued. Meanwhile, the French artillery from the first two batteries sustained their devastation on the walls of the fort, retrenched camp and the British garrison. This exchange of pounding on each other's emplacements was continuous until approximately four o'clock in the afternoon.

Suddenly, Indian and Canadian troops were spotted in great numbers around the entrance to the road to Fort Edward, and the constant small arms fire directed at the retrenched camp seized. Making a wide sweep around the fort marched a large battalion of French regulars who followed the Canadians and Indians down the road. This movement excited the British, and officers began to give orders.

Colonel Monro came out of his tent and directed officers to report to their regiments. Sergeants and corporals began to form their men on their lines of defense. The entire garrison was turned out. Charles and his fellow carpenters were placed on the flank of Frye's Regiment.

Lieutenant Bradford limped over to their position while attempting to buckle on his sword belt. "Sergeant Nurse, you have command of the squad. Ensign Greenleaf and I are being placed with the artillery temporarily. See to it that your men are readied for battle. We don't know for sure, but either the French are preparing for a final assault and we must defend ourselves, or Webb's relief column is finally coming, and we will have to sortie out and give them covering fire from the woods."

Charles saluted the Lieutenant and turned to his men. "I want each of you on this line three deep," said Charles as he issued orders. "Fix your bayonets, make sure all your gear is on and that you are ready to follow me immediately." The men quickly did as ordered.

The order came down from Colonel Frye's Regiment to load their muskets. Charles yelled to his men, "prime and load."

A terrible waiting game began. Would the enemy burst from the woods and charge headlong into the British defenses? Would Charles and his men and the British garrison be ordered to march into the road and woods and lay down fire to help a relief column get into the British camp? Either way, there would be a great many men killed and wounded.

The men stood poised for anything. The stress of the past five days with little sleep, the continued bombardment and the thunder of their own cannons were taking their toll. The men were shaking. Just before sundown, the French regulars marched out of the woods and around the flank of the British positions and returned to their own lines. Seeing this, half of the British garrison was ordered to stand down but with their arms. For some reason the incident had been relieved.

That evening, Colonel Monro sent Lieutenant Williamson outside the fort to examine the damage done by the enemy guns. He reported back that though the fort remained defensible, there was more than three feet of timbers missing as a result of enemy artillery shots on both the northeast and northwest bastions of the fort. He reported that some of the casemates in the fort's walls had received great damage as well.

Charles and his men were told to stand down. He had not written home since the siege began. Even though cannons were firing and shells bursting, he found a spot near the west wall of the retrenched camp where he sat under a cart and penned some words.

My dearest Mary,

I do not know if you have received word yet at home but I was moved up to Fort William Henry with a group of carpenters. The next day after arriving, this fort came under attack. The French have been shelling and cannonading us now for three days straight. They are attempting to beat our fortifications to the ground.

You would not recognize this place today. The enemy has knocked three feet off the top of the bastions and their shells are blowing holes in the walls of the fort. There is a retrenched camp here where we had part of the camps and redoubt that you would remember from the Battle of Lake George. If it were not for the exploding shells that threw metal upon us from the sky, we would fare better than those garrisoned in the fort.

Most of us have not slept in days now. I have never been so scared as I am now with the bombs continually exploding, men yelling and crying, the choking smell of gunpowder, dirt and blood, the lack of full rations of food. We have only ventured out to attempt to push back small attacks or sorties of the enemy, usually with results of the death or wounding of more of our men. If this was not enough most of us have no tents and it is hot during the day and cold at night.

The enemy is employing their savages to do their bidding. They have kept us under a constant small arms fire for five days. We dare not look over our walls without having lead and wood splinters thrown in our faces. There is a constant flow of wounded men to the surgeons. They have made a temporary hospital in the casemates of the fort, as there is no safer spot. They not only must treat the wounded but also the pox victims and other distempers.

Lord Jehovah, I know not if I will make it from this predicament. I pray every day with my utmost that a relief column will arrive, but to no avail. My darling, I love you and I know our child will be just like you. You must be strong. If I do not make it from here you can count on my parents. I hate to scare you, but I am not optimistic about the survival of many of us. I cannot write any more for the enemy is increasing its bombardment on our camp. I will give this letter to Thomas Greenleaf and a copy to an officer of Colonel Frye's Regiment. In case I do not make it, one of them will see that this is delivered to you.

I love you my darling,
Yours Affectionately,
Charles

DAY SIX ⁓ *Surrender* ⁓

Very early this next morning, Colonel Monro called a Council of War. Charles and John Bush were both asked to assist in taking notes at the officer's meeting. They entered the large marque tent where the meeting was to be held and took locations in the back of the tent, preparing to write. Officers began arriving. In attendance were Lieutenant Colonel Monro, Lieutenant Colonel Young of the 60th, Colonel Frye of Massachusetts, Colonel Parker of New Jersey, Lieutenant Colonel Gough of New Hampshire, all the captains of the regulars and Captain Arbuthnot of Massachusetts.

Monro began, "Gentlemen, we have information that we must review and make a decision from. First, I have received a report that the enemy has finished their third battery placed at less than 150 yards from the west wall of the fort. This places that battery so prominent that if they commence firing from it at the fort and retrenched camp that it will do more damage than both their other batteries combined. Our walls will be breached in less than a day.

"I have also received word from our artillery duty officer that we have exploded another mortar, killing thirteen men. This leaves us with a total of five small cannons, all running out of ammunition.

"All our communications with Fort Edward have been disrupted since the third, with the exception of General Webb's letter that the French had the good fortune to capture. As we can see from its contents, General Webb has no intention of sending a relief column soon."

Satisfied with Monro's defense, the officers of the Council asked that an officer be sent to the French to sue for terms.

Colonel Frye stated, "The Massachusetts men are quite wore out and would stay no longer. They would rather be knocked in the head by the enemy as stay to perish behind the breastwork."

Monro's reply was thus, "Till now, your Massachusetts men behaved and did their duty better than either the Jersey and Hampshire men, who could never be brought to do their duty with regularity or resolution. The Jersey and Hampshire men in the fort behaved scandalously when they were to fire over the parapet; they lay down upon their faces and fired straight up in the air.

"It is settled then. Before we are endowed with more casualties and the opening fire of the new battery, I shall draw up papers and have them sent with an officer to take to the enemy and seek terms of capitulation. I dissolve this meeting. See to your men and we will see what terms we will receive."

At six o'clock in the morning, a white flag of truce was raised over the fort. The cannons on both sides became silent. At approximately six thirty, Captain Rudolphus Faesch left the gates of the fort with a white flag of truce. He marched toward the closest French battery with a drummer and fifteen grenadiers. Several enemy guards stopped him, and an officer came out and met Faesch. He was then led through the French lines down to the enemy encampment and Montcalm's tent. Shortly after, Lieutenant Colonel Young of the 60th followed from the fort on horseback. He had been wounded and could not walk to the negotiations.

The officers took seats offered to them in the French general's tent. Niceties were exchanged, and then they got down to the business at hand: how would the English get out of their situation and still save further deaths and humiliation? The French needed to take full possession of the fort as well as not put further strain on their government's financial woes with thousands of prisoners.

"Sir, Lieutenant Colonel Monro has sent me to request that you reconsider offering us terms. We have attempted to continue our defense but now are under the opinion that we must capitulate now. If you can be so generous," requested Lieutenant Colonel Young.

"I understand your predicament, sir. I saw the need for your surrender days ago when I sent my aide to offer such. You have done your officers, your country and your king honor with your defense of this fort. You have done all that could have been asked of you, short of giving all your lives. I agree that you should be offered terms. I believe you should be given the same favorable terms as those given the British defenders of Minorca in 1756. Monsieur Bougainville, would you have the articles of capitulation drawn up?"

"I shall, sir," answered Bougainville, as he left the tent to draw up the papers.

Montcalm had refreshments brought for the men while they waited and talked.

"One item that we are bothered with, sir, is that of your natives. Are you going to be able to hold them to these terms?" asked Faesch.

"I believe so, but let us call a general council of my natives and their interpreters and read to them the terms. This may place them in a better spirit and accept them as their own as well," reassured Montcalm.

The chiefs and interpreters of the many tribes were convened and Montcalm addressed them. In attendance was Lieutenant Colonel Young. Montcalm started by bestowing thanks to the all the natives who had helped in the defeat of the British. Then he had Bougainville read the terms of capitulation with the natives' interpreters who did their best to translate the items to the chiefs. The chiefs seemed receptive and referred to themselves as French allies, not completely under French control. This left Montcalm wondering if his message had truly been translated in its entirety. The chiefs agreed to the terms and stated they would restrain their young warriors. Montcalm told them that personal effects of officers and soldiers were to be respected, and that all military stores belonged to the French King. The natives still reserved the right to pillage the fort and camp after the English had left.

Shortly after the Indian Council, the representatives of the two armies signed the articles, and Lieutenant Colonel Young and Captain Faesch returned to the fort. Colonel Monro had them read to the officers of the garrison.

"First, gentlemen," addressed Colonel Monro. "I want you to know that you have served your country with honor and that everything in our powers was done to see to it that this fort was not lost. Unfortunately, the enemy has superior artillery to ours and we are not able to receive a timely reinforcement without jeopardizing Albany and the entire western territories of the colonies. The French have been generous and have granted us honorable terms. Lieutenant Williamson, will you read the Articles of Capitulation."

Article 1. The garrison of Fort William Henry and the troops that are now in the retrenched camp adjoining thereto shall march out with their arms, drums beating, colours flying, and the other honours of war, with the baggage of the officers and soldiers only. They shall retire to Fort Edward under escort of a detachment of the French troops, and some of the officers or interpreters attached to the savages, early tomorrow morning.

Article 2. The gate of the fort shall be delivered up, soon after ye signing the capitulation, to the troops of His Most Christian Majesty, and the retrenched camp immediately after the departure of His Britannic Majesty's troops.

Article 3. All the artillery, warlike stores, provisions, and in general everything, except the effects of the officers & soldiers, as is already specified in the first Article, shall be faithfully delivered over to His most Christian Majesty's troops, and for this effect, there shall be given in with this capitulation, an exact inventory of all effects mentioned in this Article, this to extend equally to the fort, retrenchment and dependencies.

Article 4. The garrison of the fort, retrenchment and their dependencies are not to serve for the space of eighteen months from this day, neither against his most Christian Majesty's troops, or against his allies. An exact state of the troops, in which shall be comprehended the names of the field officers, the other officers, engineers, artillerists, commissaries and all employed, shall be given in with this capitulation.

Article 5. In the course of three months, shall be delivered at Carillon, all the officers, soldiers, Canadians, women or savages, taken by land since the beginning of this war, in North America (as for as that depends upon the commanding officer,) and according to the receipt which they shall receive from the commanding officer of the French troops, to whom they shall see delivered, an equal number of the garrison of Fort William Henry, will be capacitated to serve according to the comptroll, which shall be given in by the English officer, who delivers over said prisoners.

Article 6. An officer shall be given as an hostage till such time as the detachment which is given as an escort to the British troop's returns.

Article 7. All the sick and wounded that are not in a condition to be transported to Fort Edward, shall remain with the Marquis de Montcalm, who will take all possible care of them and return them as soon as they are recovered.

Article 8. Provisions for the British troops shall be issued for today and tomorrow only.

Article 9. The Marquis De Montcalm being desirous to show Lt. Col. Munro and the troops under his command every mark of respect in his power, on account of the brave and honorable defense they have made gives them a piece of cannon.

Given in the trenches before Fort William Henry
August 9th 1757, 12 o'clock
George Monroe, Lt. Col. of the 35th Regiment & commander of His Majesty's troops in and near Fort William Henry. Agreed to in the name of His most Christian Majesty according to the power vested in me by ye Marquis de Vaudruil his Governor General and Liut. General of New France.
Montcalm

"Officers in charge at the fort, prepare your men to march at noon for the retrenched camp. They are to carry all the baggage possible. All military stores are to be left. Officers in charge at the retrenched camp, have your men double the guards and be prepared for anything. We will be marching for Fort Edward tomorrow morning. Make room for the men from the fort," ordered Monro.

At noon, a detachment of French grenadiers marched up to the fort's gates. They were met there by a detachment of the British regulars. Both detachments entered the parade ground. The fort's entire garrison was formed and ready to march. There were no more soldiers on the bastions or parapets, and a few Indians began to climb up over them while slippping in the breaches in the casemates and others filtered in the gates after the French. One native walked up from behind the 60th and reached out and touched Captain Faesch's hat. Faesch, in one swipe of the back of his hand knocked the Indian to the ground. The closest four men lurched forward to guard the captain if needed, and the other Indians within sight jumped. The warrior who was knocked to the ground did not rise but rather crawled away like an injured dog. During the remainder of the ceremony, all the natives kept their distance but put fear into the heart of the British soldiers as they stared and laughed at them while eying their belongings with great interest.

The officers of both detachments ordered forward color guards that marched up to the flagstaff. The British guards lowered the King's colors and folded the flag; the French guards raised the flag of King Louis. After an exchange of salutes, Lieutenant

Colonel Young, who was on horseback, turned and gave an order, "Captain Faesch, form for march to the retrenched camp."

"Sir," was Faesch's reply with a snappy salute. "Company commanders, form front, to the right wheel, march!"

The soldiers wheeled from lines into columns of six abreast and began to march out the gate.

MARCH TO FORT EDWARD?

As the soldiers marched out the fort gate, more Indians began to pour in: some squeezing by the British, others climbing in the gun embrasures of the fort walls. They began to run everywhere looking for loot, in and out of the buildings, searching every inch of the fort. The British began to hear cries and yells. Even before the last of the British garrison had left the parade ground, one Indian burst open the door to the lower casemate that was used for the hospital. He began running about, yelling and parading around a man's head. He was obviously pleased with his prize holding it high above his own head, blood running from his trophy covering his arm and chest. They had found the sick and wounded. The men in the rear of the British column were terrified as they left the fort. More French soldiers rushed into the fort. Seeing the atrocities being performed by the Indians, the French forcibly took up positions in the fort, stopping the barbarity to the thirty sick and forty wounded British who had been left under French care.

As the British marched toward the retrenched camp, Indians surrounded their column with the idea of malice in their eyes but without acting on it. Many eyed the officer's baggage being carried in several wagons.

The column marched quickly into the retrenched camp, hoping for its safety. It did not take long though, and Indians began to mount the retrenchment walls terrifying everyone within. Officers attempted to order them off but this had no effect, and the natives began to enter and cause havoc.

Charles and his men were along the eastern wall. They watched the fort's garrison enter the retrenchment and saw the terror on some of their faces. Several Indians climbed over the wall near them and began to paw Charles and his friends' belongings. They pushed the Indians' hands away. Ensign Greenleaf walked directly over to one of the heathens, placing his chest against that of the Indian and yelled, "You bloody bastard, keep your stinking hands off my men or I'll kill you with my bare hands!" The Indian just grinned at Greenleaf for a moment then walked farther down the wall.

Shortly after, the Frenchman, Bougainville, arrived at the retrenched camp. Seeing the mayhem beginning, he dispatched several hundred French guards to the British camp. Thinking the show of French force would stop the natives, he ordered his men to place themselves throughout the camp. This did very little as more Indians entered the walls and began plundering small items. The British officers, worrying about barbarous attacks, ordered their men not to fight back and to surrender small items.

"Colonel Monro, I believe that if the Indians get to your officers' liquor or the rum of your soldiers, they will become intoxicated and matter will be made severely worse," stressed Bougainville.

"I agree, sir," stated Monro. He turned about to a junior officer and ordered, "Lieutenant Hamilton, have a squad of your 35th stove the barrels of rum in the storehouse and in that third wagon." Then addressing his field officers Monro said, "Make sure all liquors are destroyed that you men have. This includes your personal quantities as well."

Much of the liquor was destroyed but the Indians were quick to learn that many of the soldiers carried rum mixed in their canteens. Many officers also carried flasks with alcohol. Many savages were imbibing despite British attempts to do away with the spirits.

Things became so intense that Bougainville sent for Montcalm who arrived and ordered many of the interpreters and officers of the Indians to the retrenched camp. With the assistance of the interpreters, Montcalm attempted to squelch the riotous behaviors to the natives. He did not want another massacre like the one at Fort Oswego the previous year. He tried talking to the Indians and even threatened them. Finally, he was able to calm them slightly and, using his soldiers and the Indian officers, partially contained the Indians.

By this time, the British officers were feeling slightly safer and wanted to thank Montcalm and his officers for the terms offered. This too was a chance for the British officers to show off what they felt was a superior gentile behavior. They asked the French officers to join Monro and his officers for refreshments. This was not surprising behavior in this day and age's as required by military etiquette.

It did not take long, and chairs were brought from the wagons for all the officers. Tables were unloaded and arranged with linens, and military orderlies filled the tables with delicacies: fine foods, known only to officers, for a frontier fort with fine wine, liquors and beer to wash it down.

"Gentlemen," began Colonel Monro as he raised his glass, "it is with great modesty and honor that I and my military family bring you this final superb meal here at Fort William Henry. We are pleased with the honor of having at our table the victors of this past week's war here on Lake George. I propose a toast to General Montcalm and his loyal officers."

All the British and French officers raised their glasses and drank to the French officers.

Most of the soldiers of the British garrison were busy with their own fears and worries about the Indians continuing their pilfering of their belongings. Many were also undoubtedly worrying too if there would be more bloodshed before they marched for Fort Edward.

Many natives were still within the retrenched camp. They were continually lingering about still looking for loot. All the while the officers' tables were being arranged, and the wonderful food and drinks being served, the natives were obviously taken back by the extravagance. The chiefs of the several tribes, with sight of the officer's feast, appeared greatly disturbed that they, the French's allies, were not invited. This, to the natives, was an obvious betrayal.

Then the Marquee de Montcalm stood and spoke.

"Fellow officers, I, too, would like to give a toast to our brave British opponents. You have done your country and your King great honor. You have defended this fort with everything granted to you and suffered honorable losses of great men in the fight to protect your lands here in North America. It has been my pleasure to have such worthy enemies. I, as well, wish to thank all of you for this fine entertainment this afternoon. I have never had the pleasure of such a fine display of food and drink in the wilderness. To King George's officers," spoke Montcalm graciously.

For several hours the officers enjoyed each other's company. Seeing the delicacy of the Indian relations, Montcalm excused himself and again talked to his native allies in and around the retrenched camp through their interpreters and officers. Thinking that the natives were calming, Montcalm again met with Colonel Monro and some of his officers.

"It appears now that we shall be able to clear the natives from your camp. I believe that it would be more prudent if for your army would march tonight between eleven and twelve, rather than tomorrow morning. I will have 400 of my men here to escort you. Just to make sure all is well, I will come back to your camp just prior to your departure," expressed Montcalm.

It was decided and Montcalm left around nine that evening.

Even though the Indians were removed from the camp they were continually skulking around the walls: hundreds of them, prowling, peering and intimidating the British. Most of the men did nothing that evening but sit under arms around their fires, shivering, worrying and thinking about their predicament.

Montcalm arrived back at the British camp very late that night.

"I have been talking to some of my field commanders and the officers of the natives. We have come to a conclusion that it may not be a good idea for you to march tonight. One reason comes from thinking about what happened at the fall of your Fort Oswego, that it may not be a good idea to move prisoners until the natives have been satisfied. The results there were tragic. I will not have that here," said Montcalm.

So, Montcalm left once more and the British departure was placed again in the morning. But shortly after, a French officer arrived at the British camp with orders for Monro and his army from the Marquee de Montcalm.

"The General has received word from some of the western natives, the Huron, that your General Johnson is approaching with his natives to relieve Fort William Henry. They must not be aware of your surrender. Because of this information, General Montcalm has told me to instruct you that you must march at midnight. He will send you a guard of 200 of his grenadiers," ordered the Frenchman.

The entire camp, still packed, formed to march at midnight. This was a terrifying night, having suffered from fright all day, the intimidations of the Indians and now a midnight march into the darkness of the woods. First to leave the retrenchment were the grenadiers of the 35th Regiment, followed by the 60th grenadiers and then the regular regiments. Just fifty to sixty rods out of the camp, Captain Trice, commanding the grenadiers of the 35th, halted the column. They waited for a moment. No guards were to be seen. Then a single Frenchman, a messenger, walked up the front of the column. He addressed Captain Trice.

"A large group of the natives are not in their camps. Many of them are in the road leading to your Fort Edward. It is believed they know of your departure and intend on attacking you on the march."

Captain Trice sent this message back to Lieutenant Colonel Monro, and all were brought back into the camp once more. Here, everyone was ordered to sleep on his arms. The fires were built up and kept up all night, and the guards were increased to half the British force. Shortly after arriving back at camp, the Indians appeared, once again, all around the walls and remained there to continually intimidate them.

Charles and his men crowded about one of the fires, cold and scared.

"I don't understand why Fort Edward hasn't sent us help?" questioned Jonathan Bailey.

"Take it easy, Bailey," reassured Corporal Peirce.

"I have been west in Massachusetts and New Hampshire, and I even once went into New York up the Mohawk River a spell, but in all my travels I've never seen Ingins like some of the ones here with these Frenchmen. I had one of those grenadier Frenchmen, who could speak some English, tell me that some of them Ingins were from some huge lakes from the country called Ohia," complained Jonathan Rogers. "Some of them is down right scary, with their paint and feathers and such. Their eyes seem to drill though a man, and I wouldn't be surprised if some of um would eat ya, just as soon as a prized cow, given the chance."

"Lord Jehovah Jon, it's bad enough having to sit here and keep your own brain from running away with thoughts of what could happen, let alone have you fill it with your nightmares," said Billy Warren in a shaky voice.

"I think that in the morning everything will work out for the best," said Lieutenant Bradford. He was slouched over in a chair with his right leg up, attempting to ease the pain of his leg wound. "I am hoping that we will get on the road to Fort Edward early around daybreak and should be there by mid to late afternoon. General Montcalm does not want us to be attacked by his Indians like at Oswego; he'll make sure we have a proper guard."

"I've penned a letter to my wife, just in case something happens. I promised I'd give it to you, Thomas. Just in case something happens to me tomorrow, you must take it to Mary." Charles handed the letter to Thomas.

"I'll make sure to get it to her Charles," replied Thomas. "But, there is nothing going to happen tomorrow; that is unless Roger's Indian nightmares come true."

Charles left the fire for a few moments. He was really worried about getting out of this predicament. He walked over to where some of Colonel Frye's men were along the wall.

"Ensign," said Charles to John Maylem. They had gotten to know each other some from the various duties of the camp. "I have a favor to ask of you. In case something would happen, and I could not make it back to my wife would you deliver this letter to her?" He asked pulling the letter from the pocket of his coat. "Her name is Mary and our home is in Amesbury."

"I can do that for you, Nurse," replied Maylem. "I believe I'll be handing it back to you though at Fort Edward tomorrow."

Charles then returned to the fire with his friends. His heart was the lowest it had ever been. He did not know what the rest of the night would bring, let alone the next day.

Here continued the British garrison, a seventh night without sleep, terrified.

PLUNDER, SCALPS AND PRISONERS

Orderly drummers beat early that next morning arousing the few men who had drifted into sleep the past night. The men were still packed and were forming to parade just before five o'clock in the morning. Just as quickly as the soldiers formed, Indians climbed the retrenchment walls and began searching and pawing everyone's belongings. They had a much more severe look of malice this day, every native having a hatchet, axe or spear: their tools of death. They had not reaped much from plundering the fort the day prior, and after the nighttime attempted departure the Indians were not about to lose out this day also. Though molesting all, they seemed to concentrate on officer's belongings.

As the British column was preparing to step off, a small guard of French regulars arrived at the British camp and stationed themselves to flank the gate on the western wall that led to the Fort Edward Road.

"Column, to the front, by the left wheel, March," ordered Lieutenant Colonel Young.

Out marched the grenadiers of the 35th under the command of Captain Trice. The Royal Artillery, commanded by Captain Furnis, marched next. According to the Articles of Capitulation, the surrendering army, as a point of honor, kept a piece of artillery; consequently, Furnis and his detachment moved forward with a single brass cannon and limber being pulled by horses. Continuing in line of march were the field command officers, the 60th grenadiers, the rest of the 35th and 60th regiments and the Independent companies. The small French guard also formed on the flanks of this portion of the British column.

Indians began to filter into the ranks, confiscating any loose items. Several warriors also cut the horses from the cannon limber, liberating the animals and leading them into the woods. Officers began to be greatly harassed by the natives. Lieutenant Colonel Young of the 60th, being wounded in the siege, was getting the brunt of several natives.

"I demand that you do something about the ill treatment of my officers and men," yelled Monro to the officer in charge of the escort. "We are abiding by the Articles of Capitulation. My men are under orders not to resist the natives and not to fight anyone who approaches them. They are without ammunition and under your safety. Look at the total lack of respect and burden your savages are forcing on Colonel Young," ordered Monro as he pointed at Young. "Can you not see the ill treatment he is receiving? Can you not see that he is wounded and must be allowed to pass unmolested? Do something damn you."

"Sir, I have too few soldiers to keep all the natives from your column. I suggest that you instruct your men and officers to give up their packs. This might pacify the natives until we can march you down the road away from here and their camp," suggested the French officer. He was becoming extremely frustrated and sent a runner to General Montcalm.

Colonel Monro ordered his officers and men to give up their packs, and the Indians immediately seized as many as possible. Believing this gave them freedom to loot indiscriminately, they began to now take clothing, swords, and muskets. They even began to take the gold-laced hats of officers, to strip them of their coats, and to take pole arms of the officers and sergeants and drums from their owners.

Before the provincials could leave the retrenchment, the situation began to get severe. The night before, a guard had been placed on seventeen wounded soldiers who were not going to be able to make the march in the morning. Neither the French nor the British wanted another episode with the wounded and sick that had happened in the fort's casemates. This special guard was dismissed just as the column began to march. A group of the Indians that had now entered the retrenched camp found the wounded British and dragged them from their cots into the common area. One warrior threw his prisoner to the ground and pulling the man's head up by his hair, slashed twice with his knife, scalping the captive. The Indian lifted the blood-dripped scalp above his head and screamed in pleasure. The other natives did similar things to the rest of the wounded, all in plain sight of the provincials that were still inside the camp. These savages quickly ran out of the retrenched camp, taking their bloodied trophies with them.

"Oh God," yelled Ballard Smith. "We've got to get the hell out of here, or it'll be us next." Smith attempted to push the men in front of him to escape the camp's wall.

Charles reached in front of Smith and shoved him back in line. "Keep in line damn it. Steady men. We can't run; just keep together; and we will get out of here," reassured Charles.

Shortly, more Indians began to poor into the camp, and looting became rampant.

"Give them what they ask for. Don't resist," ordered Ensign Greenleaf. The men did as told.

The Indians began to pull men from the ranks of Frye's Regiment and force them out the gate and over the walls. One large native came from behind Charles detachment and lunged before them, hitting John Bush in the back of the legs with his club, which knocked him to the ground. Before Bush could recover and before the men around him could react, the warrior, with the help of another, grabbed John's arms and dragged him over the breastworks of the retrenchment, kicking and screaming. This made terror more personal to Charles and many of his men who had known John.

From behind them came screams: screams and yelling of women and children. The camp followers, wives and children of the regulars and some of the other colonies were under attack. Turning around, the Massachusetts men saw savages pulling the women from the camp and some ripping babes from the arms of their mothers. Other children were being swept up by savages who sprinted away as blatant kidnappers.

The provincials now marched forward leaving the camp. As they marched out the gate, one guard was tormenting soldiers by telling them what the savages were going to do to them. Just as the rear of the column exited the gates orders went out to halt and the Massachusetts men followed this order. A few ranks before Charles and his men, another friend, Jonathan Carver, was pulled from his position by three Indians who took his hat and grabbed his coat and waistcoat and then cut off the buckles of his shoes. Carver immediately sought help from the French guards.

"Help me," yelled Carver, as he pulled at the sleeves of the Frenchman. "You can't let these devils take me," he shouted as the Indians continued to try and pull him away from the French guard.

"Vous Anglais dog!" yelled the guard as he shoved Carver back in amongst the Indians who began to jab him with their spears.

Now hundreds of Indians had surrounded the entire column. Suddenly, the Indians who were in the retrenched camp came pouring out and attacked the remnants of the followers and the New Hampshire regiment in the rear of the column. With the violent actions taking place behind them and the other savagery around them, the Massachusetts Regiment became confused. Quickly the men pushed forward again, desperate and frightened.

It was only a short distance down the road that the entire provincial battalion collapsed. Men were terrified that they would be the next man killed, scalped or taken prisoner by the Indians. In an attempt to rush forward, units began banging into each other and mixing, losing all communication and command.

Ensign Greenleaf was pushed forward into the rear of Frye's rear company. He turned and yelled commands, "Nurse, Peirce, keep the men together the best you can." Greenleaf was knocked to the ground by the stampede of men.

In a wild attempt at keeping part of the men together, Charles took a risk. "Thomas, Blake, Rogers, Smith, Jones, follow me," yelled Charles as he took off running toward the southwest, away from the column. The five men broke away to follow Charles. Much of the column must have had the same inkling, for the column at this point disintegrated; part of the provincials ran straight down the road, some ran back to the camp, men like Charles and his group ran to the woods, and others made their way back to the French camp. Things now took a drastic change, for many of the natives left the column, to chase down the fleeing soldiers.

Charles turned his head to see that his men were following. Seeing a group of ten or twelve natives almost on their heals, Charles tucked his head, pushed forward as fast as his legs could carry him and bellowed, "Faster, they're almost on us."

The six men only made it about fifty yards and the Indians jumped on Charles and his men. With two to one numbers, the Indians subdued the men quickly. The savages did not beat them excessively, which surprised the soldiers. Some of the Indians began to tie up the men, others tied tethers to them and some just held them securely by the arm. Just as the Indians began to lead their captives toward their camp, General Montcalm came running with some of his officers.

The General began issuing orders to the French guard, who had done little to protect the British. They immediately began to attempt to push Indians away from men who were left in the column. Montcalm and his officers tried talking to the Indians with prisoners, which stopped Charles and his men from being dragged off by their captors. None of the Indians were willing to give up their prisoners, so Montcalm began to threaten the Indians and then attempted to make promises. Seeing that one of the closest prisoners to him was an officer, Montcalm grabbed the man. Charles knew it was Lieutenant Colonel Young's nephew. Things took a sudden change.

Thinking that Montcalm and his officers were going to confiscate all the prisoners, some of the Indians saw that they were again going to lose the chance for prisoners. One of the Indians holding Jones drew his knife and slit Jones' throat. Likewise, one of the Indians holding Smith captive bashed Smith's skull with his war club, knocking Smith to the ground, shaking uncontrollably. The heathens took the two men's scalps, this way they could at least get money for their bloodied trophy, if not for their captives. Seeing what was awry, Charles hit the closest Indian to him with his head smashing the Indians nose and kicked the other in the kneecap sending him to the ground. Charles sprinted for the woods. Thomas must have been as successful as Charles, for he too was hot on Charles' heels.

Charles and Thomas hit the woods full force, slapping and cutting though the underbrush. Without warning, Charles ran head long into a warrior knocking each other to the ground. Both Charles and the Indian got right up but Thomas was there just in time to knock the Indian in the side of his head with his musket butt. Looking behind them, the two saw three very angry Indians running directly at them with bloodthirsty eyes. They took off again on a dead run. As they ran, Charles and Thomas periodically threw any gear they had on them at their pursuers. Just as they hit a ravine, Charles yelled for Thomas to keep running. Charles dove into some bushes and when the third man came by him, he struck the Indian in the chest with his bayonet. He took off chasing Thomas and the other two Indians. Charles caught up with them as they were just cresting the next ravine and jumped on the back of the second Indian. Thomas whirled around and tripped the first one. The four men were now on the ground. Charles and Thomas were clubbing, gouging and using everything they could as weapons against the enemy. Charles went wild, pummeling the Indian with his fist until the Indian began to shake his head between shots. Without warning, the Indian swung and clubbed Charles in the forehead with his war club, throwing Charles from him. He jumped on Charles' chest and began to thrash him with the club. Fortunately, Charles was able to block many of the blows with his arms. Feeling around by his side, Charles found another weapon, grabbed it in his fist, and struck the Indian in the temple with a rock. Quivering, the Indian fell onto Charles.

Charles shoved the lifeless body off him and he ran to Thomas' aid. Taking about five large strides Charles jumped on Thomas' attacker's back and pulled him off. The three men rolled on the ground as Thomas came up on top with a knife in his hand thrusting it repeatedly into the Indian's guts. Jumping to their feet Thomas and Charles headed toward Fort Edward.

Over the next knoll, Charles caught movement to his right. He immediately dropped to the ground and motioned for Thomas to do the same. For about a half-minute they lay on the ground. It was a man. He came close enough that they could see it was Jonathan Carver. Seeing no one chasing him, they motioned for him to come over by them.

The three men knelt and crouched down catching their breath.

"I thought maybe you were dead," said Thomas to Jon.

"I thought so for a moment too, but once I got to the woods I hid out and worked my way to the south. Now I'm heading as fast as I can back to the road and to the safety of Fort Edward," huffed and puffed Carver.

"I'm not so sure the road is the way to go. If I were an Indian, I'd sit on the road and wait for soldiers running scared to death," warned Charles as he wiped sweat from his brow.

"It's not sweat, it's blood," said Thomas to Charles with concern.

"Thought I might see you two at Fort Edward, but wasn't sure if any of us were really going to get out of that mess of savages," commented Carver.

"Well I'm heading for the road," said Carver as he got up and started again northwest.

"Good luck," was Charles' comment.

Thomas and Charles waited for a few more moments and then headed out due west. They jogged about a quarter mile over a small hill and then up a mountain. This was taking most of everything they had in them. About three-quarters of the way up the mountain, it became quite rocky. It was usually common to stick as much to a trail as possible in such rocky situations but in their haste and in this type of danger they made their way as best they could. They were quite exhausted as they reached the summit.

The scream of a savage broke the forest silence. Before the men, standing regally on a rock outcrop above Charles, was a savage who in one leap knocked both men to the ground and without missing a beat jumped back on the rock while six other heathens pounced on Charles and Thomas. It was all the two men could do to block as many blows as possible, deflecting fists and clubs alike. Charles' right arm became unusable, it was broken. Within seconds the Indians had Charles and Thomas tied hand and feet and lashed to the trunk of a tree. The two stood there pinned tightly to the oak as most of the warriors sprinted off into the deep forest.

Charles and Thomas were quite bloodied. Thomas was not conscious. Charles was in great pain. Peering through a combination of blood and mucus running in his eyes, Charles watched the three remaining Indians who stood above him. Obviously, the warrior who had first assaulted them was some sort of leader. He was tall, at least six feet, and very lean and muscular. He appeared to be slightly older than most of the others, maybe in his late thirties. His bronze body was naked except for an apron of wool over his loins and leggings covering his legs. He wore tough leather moccasins on his feet. The rest of his body was covered in paint and tattoos; even his face was decorated in primitive inked symbols. Both of his ears were mutilated and pierced in multiple places, and his ear lobes hung half way to his shoulders. Around the Indian's waist, a sash held a highly ornamented tomahawk and a scalping knife. His head had been shaved or plucked in the front, leaving a long patch down the middle of his head. This was left about four inches long, which was greased to stand up like that worn by many of the Mohawks. Towards the back of his head his hair hung long, and a tuft was pulled into a crown and ornamented with a half dozen feathers, which were made to stand upright.

The Indian was intimidating as he stared at Charles. The others knelt beside him waiting his instructions. In one hand he held a large wooden club. On one shoulder he carried a quill decorated bag and powder horn, and on the other he slung a French musket. Around his neck were strung several gorgets.

The leader motioned toward Charles and Thomas. One of the savages left the others and walked over to Thomas, poured water on his head and slapped him several times to rouse him. The savage put a partial handful of parched corn in both the soldiers' mouths and likewise gave them some water. The two natives melted into the woods, leaving only the leader with the two soldiers.

Without saying a word, the tall Indian, once again, leapt from the rock outcrop. Drawing his knife, he cut the bindings on Charles and Thomas' feet and the lashing from the tree. Placing the bindings from both men's hands in his right hand, the savage bounded forward pulling the two men with him.

It was extremely difficult to keep up with the Indian, who made his way through the forest with the skills of a while tail deer. Periodically, one of the captives would trip or fall and the captor would have to hesitate momentarily while everyone regained their footing. It was easy to read the disgust on his face. They headed north, crossing the road between the two forts and continued until reaching a narrow trail. Charles was surprised when he noticed the sun poking between the trees; they were now heading west, back towards Fort William Henry. The savage stopped long enough only to give the two prisoners another drink, and they were again careening through the forest. They turned again to the north, and within several moments they burst from the woods into the open at the edge of Lake George. The Indian dragged them quickly down the shore to a group of waiting canoes just hidden from the area of the retrenched camp.

As they were arriving at the canoes, a French guard was making a fuss over a prisoner being taken to the canoes by another group of natives. It was Captain Furnis. The Frenchmen were not going to allow the Indians to take him to their canoes. They tore the officer from the native grasp and hastened toward the French camp.

Seeing this action, the Indian captor of Charles and Thomas pulled them back into the woods. He motioned for two of his fellow savages, and they came to his call. Charles and Thomas thought this was going to be the end. Thomas began to cry; Charles was too afraid to cry and just hung his head in defeat. The tall savage pulled out his knife and held it to their heads, shaving them except for a center crown of hair like his own. One of the Indians took Charles' coat and the other cut off all their other clothing, quickly ransacking them for any loot. The Indian wearing Charles' coat pulled a container from his pouch and smeared smelly grease mixed with red ochre over their heads and bodies. Disguised now as savages themselves, Charles and Thomas were dragged onto the beach and loaded into separate canoes. Charles was terrified: stunned as he sat naked in the savages' boat waiting, who knew what form of hell would dominate Charles' next days. Charles slowly looked around. Something wasn't right. There appeared to be about fifty savages in the canoes. Their appearance was quite that of a large anachronism; none of them were Indians. They were prisoners readied for transport, but to where?

THE CAPTIVES MARCH

A few other prisoners, dressed as Savages, were dragged down to the lake and put in the canoes. Within a short time, groups of savages from the forest and the area of the fort swarmed down to the canoes, climbed in and shoved off into Lake George. The Indians were as varied as the many canoes they paddled. The noble savage that had captured Charles and dragged him and Thomas to the lake was in the canoe with Charles, protecting his new property. The Indian thrust a paddle in Charles' bound hands and grunted, "ke-dje may." (You paddle) Charles wasn't sure what the words meant, but began paddling with his injured arm.

The pain was severe as Charles and the others dug their paddles into the deep blue waters of Lake George. It took what seemed like only minutes to glide across the bay and enter the main waters of the lake. Charles turned about, taking a last glance back at Fort William Henry. He could see the fort and the cleared ground around it. There was much movement, and smoke was coming from most areas of the fort and lands around it. As they paddled past the French camp, screams went up from the savages in the canoes and cheers from the French in their camp. Charles believed this might be his last glimpse of English America. His captor struck Charles in the back of the head, causing Charles to quickly jerk his head forward once again.

The flotilla of twenty native canoes wasted no time in making it to the first narrows on the lake. This spot in the lake was clogged with islands. Here, a large mountain-peninsula, jetted out into the lake. It was called Tongue Mountain because of its shape. At this point, the prisoners were given a drink, and the paddles were given to others to take their turns. Charles was greatly relieved. It only took minutes for his arm to stiffen, and the swelling caused his arm to throb in pain. Charles' captor reached forward, pulled out his knife, cut Charles' bindings, and tied his good arm to the side of the canoe. Charles lowered his injured arm into the cool water hoping that the soothing temperature would help.

Not far off, Charles caught the glimpse of a familiar face. The man, like Charles and most of the prisoners, had been stripped: head shaved and painted like an Indian. Charles stared intently, but dare not say a word. The man looked back at Charles and nodded his head acknowledging that he recognized Charles as well; it was Ensign Maylem. Now Charles felt even more defeated. Both Maylem and Thomas were captives, and none of Charles' letters would reach Mary.

Taking up paddles once more, the Indian canoes headed up the lake. Charles had been all the way up the lake to scout on the French Fort Carillon in the past, so the sights of the lake were nothing new to him. Charles knew at this point that they were, for the time being, heading towards the northern French forts. His main concern was if the savages would divert to their homelands, wherever that may be.

At sundown, the flotilla reached the second narrows, another area full of islands and a smaller peninsula that the British called Sabbath Day Point. Here the Indians stopped and took their prisoners on shore, tying them to trees. The natives left a guard on the canoes, kindled fires and sent out scouts. The remainder of the Indians ate and then sent men over to feed the prisoners. Food, again, was a meager mouthful of parched corn. Several of the prisoners were not happy about this and loudly attempted to demonstrate the treatment. One of the Indians, a large man, walked over to one of the protesters and struck the prisoner in the head with his war club, dislodging the man's lower jaw and causing blood to spray from his gaping mouth. The savage then took his club in both hands, lifted it above his head, and began to smash the prisoner's head to mush. Hearing the commotion, a group of warriors ran to the area where the prisoners were. The warrior, who had captured the man who was just killed, shoved the other Indian, and harsh words were exchanged. Prisoners were property, and the one Indian had just reduced the value of the other's booty. The owner pulled his knife and took the scalp of the dead prisoner, held it in the face of the other Indian and let out a yell. The tension now seemed to be dispersed and the savages went back to their fire. None of the prisoners could sleep this night.

Just before dawn, the prisoners were woken up and given some water and another portion of parched corn. They were then loaded into the canoes. The warrior who had captured Charles came to him and tied Charles' injured arm up with a piece of deer skin around his neck, making a kind of sling for it. The warrior cocked his head sideways and said in an almost caring tone, "au-ko-zee o-neek." (Sick arm).

The warriors finished loading, and the canoes shoved off heading north. After a few hours of paddling, the canoes reached where the lake began to end and it narrowed down to the size of a river. The natives now slowed the paddling as the waters flowed quicker. Just as the waters turned into rapids, the Indians pulled the canoes to the west shore and landed the flotilla.

A few of the warriors, those who appeared to be the leaders of the Indians, began to direct the others. All of the gear in the canoes was gathered into bundles, and straps were tied around them to make them easier to carry. Many of the prisoners were loaded down with these packs. The rest of the prisoners and part of the natives picked up the canoes in preparations to portage around the rapids. Charles was made to carry two of the Indians' bundles. The group marched overland several miles north by northwest. Much of the land was moderately flat with only a few small hills to traverse. After about two hours they reached water once more. Charles recognized it as Wood Creek. Here there were no rapids but the water was swift. The canoes were placed back in the water, bundles reloaded and everyone drank water.

By noon the flotilla was on the move again, paddling west past the French Fort Carillon. It did not take long and they passed the peninsula, turned north and made their way along Lake Champlain.

Just prior to nightfall, the canoes passed the narrows of the lake. The French had a fortification here as well. Fort St. Frederic, though in disrepair, was an imposing fort. The stonewalls and multi-story tower mounted over forty cannons and commanded the waters of the lake. The warriors did not want to waste time for the canoers kept on paddling north up the lake. The lake opened up in breadth for about a day's paddle and then widened drastically giving the flotilla a huge open route to continue forward.

After three full days of paddling, the flotilla left Lake Champlain and entered the Richelieu River. The farther north the Indians and their prisoners progressed, the more the river narrowed. The next day, the flotilla passed two other French forts. The first, Fort Ile Aux Noix, was more of the fortified island. On the east side of the island there was only about 800 feet between the island and the shore. On the west, it was about 1600 feet.

The second fort was St. Jean. At this point, the Indians unloaded their belongings and made their prisoners carry their packs. The prisoners were securely tied and put on tethers. The warriors and their prisoners began to march over the northwest, carrying their packs and canoes.

At around sun up the next morning, they reached another river; this one much larger than the Richelieu. The sun rose to Charles' left, so he knew that this must be the St. Lawrence. However, he had no idea which part of the river they had come out on.

The trail they marched on was leading to a village on the south shore. Charles could see a large island French city. The village on the south side was a visible mixture of military, religion, and savageness. Charles slowed and surveyed the village they were approaching. Closest to the river and directly on the shore, stood a stone fort. On the west stood a Papal church. Surrounding the church and what appeared to be over thirty Indian huts was a rude stockade.

From behind, Charles' captor shoved Charles, knocking him down. The savage grabbed Charles by his good shoulder and literally lifted Charles back onto his feet. The warrior pointed at the village saying, "Caughnawaga, Sault St. Louis," (Caughnawaga was the name of the Natives who lived at this site called, in French, Sault St. Louis) and jerking on Charles tether, dragged him into the gate of the stockade.

Charles was stunned as he entered the stockade. All the prisoners were kept with their masters. Those without prisoners were quick to display their scalps and trophies they had taken. As Charles scanned the village, he saw Caughnawaga women and children scurrying about and elders welcoming back warriors from the fight at Fort William Henry. Fires that were not kindled were set ablaze, and pots were filled for a feast. Charles became very concerned as he noticed scalps hanging from every hut.

A party of French officers and soldiers came from the stone fort to the village. A council between the soldiers and the warriors with prisoners ensued. After the council, about two thirds of the warriors and their prisoners were escorted over to the island city of Montreal. Charles, along with part of the prisoners, was not taken. With this, more tension was added to their predicament.

Four of the remaining prisoners at the village, including Charles, were taken to a separate area of the stockade where they were bound to poles buried in the ground. A fire was kindled in front of them and a large black iron pot of water was placed over the fire. Shock fell over Charles and the others. A group of several dozen savages came over. Several animal robes were placed on the ground, and some of the elder warriors took seats on them. Some of the youngest braves stood behind these Indians. One of the savages walked into the center of the assemblage and motioned saying, "We have taught our young warriors how to fight, how to kill a man and how to scalp him. We now must teach them how to cut a man to put aw-kick-ong (in the kettle). Obwandiyag (Pontiac), come forth and show Egushwa, your young relative, and the other young warriors how to do this."

Charles' master stood and walked into the center. This was the first Charles had heard his name. Charles said it to himself in his subconscious, "Pontiac."

Pontiac motioned to several of the younger warriors and said to Egushwa, "bring me a prisoner." The young warriors untied one of the men and dragged him over to where Pontiac stood. Charles and the other two prisoners cringed, wondering if they would be next.

The man brought over by the warriors was held with arms outstretched; he was screaming. With a swoop of his knife and two deep cuts into the captive's chest, Pontiac reached into the man's chest cavity and pulled out his still beating heart. It poured blood. The man shook uncontrollably, and his eyes rolled back into his head. Pontiac held the heart above his head, blood oozing from the openings of the heart and covering his arm. He let out a loud high-pitched whoop and lowered the heart to his mouth and took a bite of the heart. Then he handed it to Egushwa instructing him to do the same. In this way the heart was passed amongst the warriors and devoured. Reaching down and scooping a hand full of blood in the palm of his hand, Pontiac slurped the warm red blood into his mouth. Then motioning to the young warriors with his bloodied hand Pontiac asked, "ke-gus-kaw-nas-baw-gwe naw? (Are you thirsty?)", and he motioned for the young men to do as he had.

Pontiac asked another seasoned warrior to come forward to further teach the young men. "Micinac, come and teach the young ones how to further prepare this man."

Micinac came forth and looked the body over. The young warriors still had the lifeless body stretched between them. Micinac took his tomahawk and chopped, dismembering the man. After removing the man's head, he pulled out his knife and began to take slices off the man's breast, stomach and back, taking care to place them in the boiling pot. Micinac also made sure to explain the importance and the differences in taste amongst the body parts he placed within. Charles and the other men shook with fear, terror and outrage. Most turned their head in horror but the warriors held their heads forward, forcing them to watch. After the meat had some time to boil, Micinac reached into the pot with a stick pulling out a piece of flesh and chawed on it, smacking his lips. Then, wiping some of the grease from his face, he offered for the others to come forth and eat the meat.

"This is the meat of a warrior. You have eaten his heart and drank his blood. Now you eat his meat. This you have done not for nourishment but to gain his strength and courage, so you will be stronger the next time you must go into battle. This is the custom of our people, Anishinaabek (original people). You now know how to prepare a man for feast, and you now have partaken in such a feast. As with all our traditions, you will take this knowledge from the Great Spirit and pass it on to your children," lectured Micinac.

Micinac pulled another piece of meat from the pot and walked over to the other prisoners. Warriors walked behind the prisoners and forced them to open their mouths, forcing them to each take a bite of the flesh. The prisoners squirmed and jerked away, clamping down their jaws. The warriors grabbed them by the hair and putting extreme pressure on their jaws forced the prisoners' mouths open. Most of them spit out the meat but several like Charles vomited almost immediately.

Pontiac walked over to Charles and lifted Charles head up with his hand. "How can you expect to become a mush-kaw-waw (strong) warrior? You must learn to take all the strength you can from your enemy and from other warriors. It is the Great Spirit's ways. We will teach you many of our ways as you become ne-kaw-nes (my brother)," reassured Pontiac. "Ke-ne-se-to-tow naw? (Do you understand me?)"

The prisoners were left tied to the post all night. They worried and dreamed of what their fate would now be. Would they be eaten next; would these savages butcher them; would they be traded to the French? They dare not talk. From this point forward, Charles totally distanced himself from the other prisoners.

The next morning, the prisoners and a handful of others were loaded into a dozen canoes, and the group set out paddling West on the St. Lawrence River. For now, Charles and the other prisoners were safe, but they wondered where they were heading. Charles was surprised they did not head East toward Quebec.

Early in the morning, the canoes passed two separate Indian villages. For two days, the small flotilla continued, stopping only in the dark to eat and sleep a few hours. On day three and four out of Montreal they encountered many islands in the river, slowing their progress. There were also some rifts that made their maneuvering challenging.

The following two days, the flotilla did not make shore. They paddled through the narrows, passing the French outpost La Galette, a small stockade fort, and the native village Oswegachi. At the mouth of the river, a large island divided the waterway and as the flotilla passed the North side of the island they also passed the fortification of Frontenac. Frontenac was a well-established four bastioned fort. As they passed, Charles imagined, by observing the many storehouses and traffic, that this fort must be a key to the supply lines between the French Western posts and Montreal and Quebec. It was obvious the great influence the Western fur trade had on this enemy fort.

Heading due South, the flotilla of Indian canoes now entered and crossed Lake Ontario. Charles was taken back; this lake was even bigger than Lake Champlain. On the South coast they turned West and shortly passed the ruins of Fort Oswego. The buildings and what was left of the walls were in great deterioration as was the smaller Fort Ontario. Charles fidgeted in the canoe as they passed these fort ruins. He remembered the tales he had heard about the fall of these forts and the similarities of the savage cruelties to the garrison of Fort Oswego, much like what he was living through now. The savages whooped in a form of salute as their canoes passed.

The terrain changed, and for the three days it took to traverse Lake Ontario there were few mountains within sight. The flotilla kept close to the southern shore. On the morning of the fourth day, just as they noticed a large river emptying into Lake Ontario, another fort was spotted. This was another impressive fort.

Setting majestically atop a hill on the shore of the confluence of Lake Ontario and the river was a large stone three-story French castle nestled within the defensive walls of the fort. Suddenly, a shot rang out from a native firelock in a canoe behind Pontiac's, and whoops were yelled. A puff of smoke and a thudding boom of one of the fort's cannons answered. The Indians wasted no time swinging their canoes into the river and paddling hard to beach them on the East shore of the river about one hundred yards South of the fort. They quickly unloaded their packs and had their prisoners take their canoes out of the water and place them safely on shore. They could not risk leaving them in the extreme current of this river. The prisoners were loaded with their packs, and the group of savages and prisoners climbed the knoll to the fort. A party of French regulars met the Indians about half way to the fort. They exchanged words in French and were escorted into the fort. The prisoners were tied together and left under the guard of several braves. The other savages were taken to a group of officers near the large stone building.

Charles was not afraid now being in such a refined fort, even if it was one of the enemy's. It was much more impressive than the stockade forts he had seen along the route. Charles took great notice of the fort as he rested on the ground. He could see now that the large stone house was actually a two and a half story building. From his distance, across the parade ground it appeared to be somewhere about one hundred feet wide by fifty feet deep. There were minor fortifications on the lake and riversides of the fort, but on the other two sides there were major deterrents in place. To the South and East there were a ditch and a wall sloping to a wall facing the enemy's approach. There were also two earthen bastions and some outer works that Charles could not make out from where he sat. New stockade was also in place. There appeared to have been much new construction taking place. Charles surveyed, seeing new buildings for barracks, church, storehouses and another stone building with an arched roof; Charles took this for a powder magazine.

It wasn't long and the Indians came back and loaded their prisoners with their packs and marched them to the South where there was a group of Indians' bark houses. Here, the prisoners were tied to stakes beside one of the large dwellings. They were given some meager food and water. They were left outside as most of the warriors entered the largest house. It wasn't long and a group of Frenchmen arrived and entered the house also. Charles and the others could hear the savages and Frenchmen speaking. They could not understand the savages and could understand almost none of the French. It seemed that they were holding a peace council of sorts. He also learned that this fort was called Niagara.

Suddenly, it began to rain profusely. What a miserable night this turned out to be. Charles and the other prisoners lay on the bare ground in the mud and sodden earth, being pelted with rain. The temperature began to drop. Several of the native's dogs came over looking for food. Charles had a morsel of meat Pontiac had given him. He gave it to one of the dogs that he coaxed to lay on the ground by him, so he could share some body heat with the animal.

In the morning, the sun came up bright and hot, and the rain from the previous night made it very humid. The savages woke their prisoners, and they made their way back to the canoes, loaded their packs and headed South down the swift river. Paddling was more for direction rather than for movement at this place in the river. It did not take long, and the banks of the river turned into the walls of a gorge. After about five or six miles, the canoes were landed on the west bank, and the packs and canoes were carried up to the top of the gorge walls. Here they passed a small trading house. They did not stop but continued on for about three miles. At this spot in the river the party stopped and all looked over the gorge wall at a natural wonder, a huge whirlpool. It was no wonder there was a portage. Never had Charles seen such an oddity. Here they all rested and took water.

Moving on up the portage, Charles could see that the river began to fill with rapids. This was a mighty river with rock walls, and its riverbed scattered with boulders adding to the dangers. After a little while, the walls lessened and the portage trail continued along the river's edge. About several miles down river, Charles could hear a dull roaring. As they continued, it increased, as did the current and the severity of the river. Charles had seen and been on many waters, but none as dangerous as this river. The water was a deep blue-green. A great mist became visible ahead as they marched forward along the portage and the roar increased. Just as the portage turned, the greatest cataracts Charles had ever seen plummeted over the edge of the gorge into a bay below. Charles had no idea a waterfall of such magnitude existed. The Indians and prisoners stood and watched for some time. Here they took food, and the natives appeared to make an offering by throwing tobacco and some other items into the water. Charles and the other prisoners easily saw the Indian's reverence.

Less than half a mile southeast of the falls, the flotilla was put in the water once more. The river now was still wide but not ferocious as before the cataracts. They paddled around the West side of a large island and then moved South, reaching a small set of rapids that they maneuvered. They ended on another great sea, which the savages called Erie. Once on the lake, the flotilla cut due South reaching the South shore by sundown. They then turned West and paddled along the shore, taking times to rest and eat only between turns paddling.

After a day and a half of this, they passed an island, and adjacent the island and shore stood another wooden stockade French fort. They stopped on the island and rested and ate for several hours. They then headed out once more West on Lake Erie.

The land along the South shore of this large lake was very level. The foliage was tall and strong. The trees spread a rich climax forest canopy of oaks, hickory and locust. Often, Charles could see game along the shore, drinking early in the morning and evenings. As they had done before, the flotilla traveled virtually day and night, eating and sleeping in the canoes. On the fifth day, they stopped at a place the Indians called Sandusky. Around this bay and the peninsula jutting out into it, was a forest of cedar trees. The natives posted men on the canoes, and the rest of the Indians and prisoners went on shore, kindled fires, ate and slept.

Charles could tell something was different when Pontiac awoke him. The first thing the natives did was place the prisoners in the lake and wash the old paint and grease off them, and then they applied new. Looking around at the savages, Charles saw too that they had done the same, adding new paint, greasing and painting their hair, adorning their bodies and heads with silver and gold arm bands and earrings. Many also put on more decorative clothing such as leggings, breechclouts and a few put on shirts. Something was awry.

After a quick mouth full of corn and some water, the Indians loaded their prisoners in the canoes and were headed northwest across the lake. They paddled all day and night. The next morning brought them to a wide river, and Charles could tell the excitement in the Indians. As they entered the river, there were islands both to the East and West. One of the first features Charles spotted was a very large island, long and narrow. As they passed the large island Charles spotted another good sized island on the other side of the river. The Indians turned their canoes to the East side of this island. Now the terrain changed. The area on both sides of the river had been cleared. Charles knew now that they were again nearing civilization. Long narrow farms began to appear on the East of the river with small vertical log and board walls, small family dwellings. The farms continued for several miles stretching in places a mile deep. Then Charles tensed as he saw an Indian village on the West bank surrounded by a stockade, and on the East side, about a mile down the river, he spied another native village. As the canoes made it farther into the river, Charles noticed a third village, this one on the East and more of the long narrow farms and houses on both sides of the river. The canoes turned the bend in the river, and shortly Charles felt relief as he saw a sizable fort. It was well stockaded with many buildings within.

Suddenly, Pontiac stood in the canoe and let out a scream and whoop as savages in the canoes began firing their muskets into the air. From the East side of the river, almost opposite the fort, there was a return of whoops and gun firing. Cannon fire then erupted from the bastions of the fort. Charles jumped and cringed not knowing for sure if they were going to be fired on, but just then the canoes veered off to the area of the whooping and firing. It was another Indian village. The natives brought the canoes into the beach and jumped out. There was a loud exchange of yells, words, and jesters. Savages had rushed to the beach to welcome the returning warriors. Charles now was at the natives' mercy, in their own village.

THE ADOPTION

Dragging Charles behind him, Pontiac made his way through the crowd of natives, each taking turns patting the returning warriors on the back and making gestures of praise at their acquired loot of prisoners and scalps. Suddenly most of the men formed into a double line and began to taunt and make intimidating gestures to the prisoners. Pontiac and the other captors grabbed their prisoners and physically threw them into the line of molesters. The Indians began to beat Charles and the other captives with sticks, fists and clubs. Pontiac and others motioned for them to run through the gauntlet. Charles began to sprint forward. After a few steps he was struck in the head. Stunned, he staggered forward and dropped his head. Then he was struck in the leg with a war club bringing him to his knees. The Indians began to pummel him with fists, he dragged himself to his feet once more and staggered forward. Toward the end of the line, Charles was bashed square in the forehead by another club, and he flew backwards onto his back. The few belongings he had were strewn on the ground. Now, many of the women of the tribe lined up and began poking Charles and the other prisoners with sticks. One woman, unseen by Charles, knelt down quickly and picked up his belongings.

Charles regained his footing and being very dazed reached the end of the gauntlet. His back was gashed in several places and he was exhausted. Pontiac again took Charles' tether and led him into a crowd of women. Pontiac approached the group and yanking hard on the tether, pulled Charles to the ground at the feet of the women. Charles let out an excruciating groan and gasped as he hit the ground. The women before him began to chuckle at the site of the naked white man before them. Pontiac kicked Charles in the ribs and, pulling Charles by the tether, handed the leather cord to one of the women, Me-no-pe-boon (Pleasant Winter). Pontiac explained, "He is your property. Your husband, Mis-ko wau-bo-yon (Red Blanket) has not returned with us. He died as a great warrior and has brought the blessings of the Gichi Manidoo upon you and your family. He killed many white men before his life was taken. Take this man and adopt him into your life replacing Red

Blanket. Teach him what is expected of him; teach him our ways, and make him your husband and the father of your children."

Pleasant Winter broke down in tears, raising her hands to the sky and beginning to wail. The other women around her began the chants to the Great Spirit for her loss. They attempted to comfort her. The eldest of the women took the tether from Pleasant Winter's hand and pulled on the leather bringing Charles back up to his feet. She dragged him to a pole outside one of the large bark houses and tied Charles securely beside several dogs.

That night there was great feasting and dancing among the Ottawa. Charles could not sleep. The eerie shadows of the Indians leaping and prancing about a great fire conjured up fright and demons in the depth of Charles' subconscious. He shook with fear awaiting his fate. Finally, ever so late, he drifted off into a sleep of total exhaustion.

Charles was startled into full awareness by a drenching of ice-cold water thrown on him by the old woman. Charles sprang to his haunches like an animal awaiting danger. The old woman chuckled at Charles and chattered at him in a commanding tone. Charles lowered his head in subordination, and she made her way toward the river.

Charles shook his head, arms and shoulders like a dog attempting to dry himself and shake himself into full consciousness. He scanned his surroundings. Charles appeared to be on a grand avenue in the center of the Indian village. Rows of large bark huts stood on each side of the avenue. There were two large fire areas of six fire pits each. Charles counted over a dozen huts or longhouses, mostly parallel to the river in the row closest to the river. Two other individual huts were very close to the river. One large hut closest to the fire areas appeared to be for something special, maybe for ceremonies. On the opposite side of the avenue Charles counted more than a dozen more long houses, most oriented toward the center avenue and river with a large fire pit area on each flank. The houses appeared to be dwellings for multiple families. Each house was constructed of long poles tied together and covered by large pieces of bark stitched together. There was an opening at each end covered by a hide, and there were several holes in the roof for ventilation of smoke. Most of the buildings were massive, reaching one hundred feet in length.

To the North, across the river, and to the West there were many long narrow farms with quaint cottages, many of board and batten and some plastered exteriors. East of the village fields of corn, beans, and squash stretched nearing their harvest-time. A fine fort with stockades stood almost directly across the river. The fort had four regular corner bastions, and atop a pole flew a large French flag that snapped lively in the stiff breeze. Charles estimated the stockade at 600 feet by 400 feet.

As Charles surveyed the village, more of the inhabitants began to mill about. Many of the women began to tend the fires. From the longhouse closest to the pole Charles was tied, emerged Pleasant Winter. She walked directly to Charles and asked, "ke-gus-kaw-naw-baw-gwe naw?"

Charles could not understand.

Pleasant Winter raised her eyebrows, cupped her hand and held them to her mouth and asked again, "ke-gus-kaw-naw-baw-gwe naw?"

Charles thought he now understood and nodded his head. Pleasant Winter walked to a large barrel and filled a dried gourd hanging on the barrel. Walking to Charles, she handed him the gourd. Charles bowed his head in thankfulness and quickly drank the water. Then Pleasant Winter walked to the closest fire. She bent over a bark basket and placed some food in a smaller one. Returning to Charles, Pleasant Winter made a motion for Charles to eat as she handed him the small basket. He was starving and devoured the venison, corn and beans in the basket.

After a short time, many of the women walked into the adjacent fields. Pleasant Winter untied Charles' tether from the pole and led him into the field. She knelt down and tied Charles' tether to her own ankle. Pleasant Winter grabbed an ear of maize pulling it off the stalk. She turned to Charles and said as she put the maize into a basket, "ke-te-gaw-nes, you work."

Charles was stunned; she spoke some English. Pleasant Winter tugged his tether and waved her hand motioning for him to help. She began again to collect maize and Charles, realizing he was to work, began to harvest the corn as well.

For several weeks Charles was taken to work harvesting crops, skinning animals, tending the fires and fetching water and wood. He had made no attempts to escape, but he had made great efforts to observe his surroundings, his captors, and to learn some of the native language.

The women and Pleasant Winter had become comfortable with Charles. Much of the time he was not tethered. At night he was always tied. The women saw no threat from Charles and were impressed with his knowledge of crops and of harvest, which was normally women's work in their culture. Pleasant Winter had even been allowing her children to play with Charles, and they began to look forward to their time with him.

Part of Charles' assimilation into the Ottawa was delivered in story telling by elders. Charles was escorted to the large council house one day. Within, already seated, were many of the male elders and warriors of the tribe. Charles recognized Pennahouel, Ego-me-nay and Aonssik. There were several visiting Ottawa from a far off land of L'Arbre Croche. These men were introduced as Nissowaquet and Micmac, who Charles remembered from Montreal. A Frenchman, Charles Langlade, from a much northern fort, Michilimackinac, escorted these two. One of Langlade's interpreters, Fleurimont Herbin Abbe' Matavet, sat beside Charles and translated in broken English with his heavy French accent. Ne-saw-key, one of the head elders rose and addressed the others.

"Our people, the Anishinabek, first met Wemitigojiwuk (French or les Francais) at the mouth of the French River. Monsieur Champlain was looking for furs. Our ancestors offered him thick le castor (beaver). For many years we have traded with les Francais. We have trusted many of these men, and many like Monsieur Langlade come and live with us and take our women for wives. They understand our way of life and bring us presents.

"For many years our ancestors fought the Iroquois. Our fathers les Francais helped us. They traded weapons for our furs. We also joined with the Ojibwe, Nipissing and Wyandot.

"For nearly one hundred years we have warred with the Iroquois, but then les Francais and Zhaaganaash (Anglais, Englishmen) began to fight. Les Francais convinced the Ottawa to help them fight the Anglais. They had two wars. During the second, les Francais sent Monsieur Cadillac from Michilimackinac to build a fort at the River de'troit (strait, Detroit). Cadillac invited our people to move and build our village near his Fort Pontchartrain. Our ancestors did this as did the Wyandot. Some of the Ojibwe also moved South to Saginaw Bay.

"Les Francais fought a third war with the Anglais. Many of us traveled far East to Quebec. Les Francais thought the Anglais were going to attack them, but they did not. While many of us were at Quebec, Pontiac led our remaining warriors in a war against other western tribes.

"Now the Ottawa are once more helping les Francais in a war against the Anglais. Two years ago we fought in a great battle against a great Anglais warrior, Braddock. Pontiac again led our tribe East to the forks in the great rivers. Then they went to the land of the Iroquois, that the Anglais call New York. We attacked a large Anglais camp on Lake St. Sacrament. We saw many Anglais killed; we saw their Fort William Henry burned. Our warriors have returned with many scalps and captives.

"Our history with Les Francais has been long. This war proves to be too long. I believe our father, King Louis, will soon be asking us once again to help them. Our harvest is good. Hunting parties must go out if we are to survive this winter. We must begin to think if we will fight with our brothers, Les Francais, next summer. We must prepare for the snow to come and then hold new councils."

Charles was taken back to his lodge where he was served a feast of roasted meat, maize, squash, and berries. Afterward, Pleasant Winter asked Charles to sit and talk with her in the woods near the edge of the camp.

"We have been watching you and believe that you are accepting us as family," said Pleasant Winter. "The other women are also impressed with your hard work in the fields. The men who saw you shoot when you were captured are equally impressed, but it is not time for you to be given a weapon to hunt, maybe next season. We the ones who make decisions, the council of women, have given permission for you to accompany our men hunting. There is plenty of work to be done on the hunt, and you can be trusted with them to venture away from the village now."

The wheels began to turn in Charles' mind. This could be his chance to escape, his way to return to his real family; but he must follow along and wait for the most perfect timing. He must not let on that he intends to escape and must make all think he is assimilating into the tribe and his adopted family, at all costs.

Pleasant Winter then continued on a more personal emphasis. "The women have given you a name, Ke-te-gay we-ne-ne. This means farmer. You are among the best in our tribe."

"I am pleased, me-gwetch (thank you). Those of your tribe have treated me with kindness and respect. Your customs are much different than my people's," responded Charles. "I have become very worried though that I will not ever see my family again," he said with great remorse.

Pleasant Winter reached forward and stroked Charles' hair to reassure him. "You are with your new family now. I am your aw-guay (woman)."

Charles did not understand that she had taken him as her husband; he only understood she was attempting to comfort him.

Pleasant Winter continued. "You are now a member of the Anishinaabe. We believe that the Gichi Manidoo (Great Spirit) places everything before us in four stages. The Gichi Manidoo has given us four seasons. Zeegwuna (Spring) is in the East and is the place of great spiritual understanding. The eagle represents it. This is when we make much maple sugar. Neebing (Summer) is in the South and is the place of innocence like the robin. We plant our maize, beans, peas and pumpkins in early Neebing. Dagwagina (Fall) is in the West where one contemplates all thought. This is also where the buffalo lives. This is the harvest season and much work. Beboong (Winter) is in the North. It is the place of great wisdom like the bear. This is when we remain in our longhouses and meditate.

"Our people also believe there are four parts to our lives; infancy, youth, adulthood and old age. All of these are interlinked and one must experience all four to live a truly balanced and full life."

Charles began the next day to accompany some of the men on hunting trips. They would be gone for two to five days at a time. The men usually ventured North. By mid-November, Charles was quite accepted on the hunts and thought of as a great help.

About once a week, men of the tribe paddled across the river to the fort to barter for goods or negotiate with the French officers for presents. There was a continual attempt to negotiate alliances.

When Charles accompanied any of the Ottawa chiefs he was treated as an equal at the fort. If he was not with the chiefs, Charles usually stayed in the background and quietly observed.

It did not take long, and Charles learned the fort was called Fort Pontchartrain. He also learned the names and backgrounds of some of the French officers. Jacques-Pierre, sieur de Danean de Muy was commandant of the fort. Muy was born in Quebec in 1695. He had joined the army as an Ensign at age fifteen. Muy, now at age sixty-two, was a Captain and had been commandant of five different posts. Lieutenant Jean Baptiste Henry Beranger was Muy's second in command. Charles counted a garrison of approximately thirty-five uniformed Frenchmen.

There were many more militia within and around the fort who periodically served under Muy. Charles estimated there could be several hundred. Captain Laurence Eustache Gamelin commanded these militiamen. Garmelin was a longtime resident of the area.

Periodically, the militia would be augmented with men from the other close garrisons. Most often, and visiting here most, was Sieur Charles Michel de Langlade from the Northern French post of Michilimackinac. Langlade, twenty-eight, was born at Michilimackinac. His father was a French fur trader there, and his mother an Ottawa. He, like his father, also married an Ottawa woman. Now, in 1757, Langlade had remarried a woman from Montreal. He had begun his career as a warrior at the tender age of ten. In the past decade, Langlade joined the French army and now was an Ensign and performed duties as Indian agent, second in command at Michilimackinac and often was placed in charge of warriors, especially Ottawa, on raids and war parties. He was one of Pontiac's closest allies.

Langlade and several others had warned the Ottawa about taking their captives away from their villages. Captain Muy had also made several attempts at purchasing Charles and others from the natives.

Several Ottawa prepared to leave on a long two-week hunt. They were hoping to kill several moose or bear. Charles was to accompany them. They were traveling to the large bay, Saginaw, several days North up the great lake. The men were hoping to travel by canoe, and that evening the canoe was loaded with supplies for the next morning's departure.

Charles could tell there was a difference around Pleasant Winter and her family. The food was more plentiful; Charles was given a new heavy-woolen-blanket coat for the trip, and Egushwa presented Charles with his own knife for skinning the animals.

Charles ate everything put before him and even put some extra into his haversack before loading it into the canoe. When he returned to the longhouse, Pleasant Winter picked up a small leather bundle and handed Charles a large bear hide. She took him by the hand and led him out the back door of the hut into the woods. Just inside the wood line there were a large beach tree log and an uprooted hemlock leaning over it. In the hollow from the hemlock's root ball, Pleasant Winter spread out the bear hide. She sat on the hide and motioned for Charles to join her.

"The items in that package are yours. I have kept them for you knowing how important they were to you. Open them. I believe your new family ties here are now strong enough for you to get these back," said Pleasant Winter in a soft voice.

Charles carefully unwrapped the leather from around the items. Tears welled up in his eyes, and he made a gulping noise.

"You dropped them that first day here at our village. While you were being beaten, I scurried over and scooped them up. They looked important," explained Pleasant Winter.

Charles gained his composure and held up the pocket watch his father had given him. "This is my grandfather's. My father gave it to me when I left for war. It tells time," stated Charles proudly. "And this," Charles hesitated as he leafed through the pages. "This, my mother gave me. It has words, important words on the pages for my children to hear some day."

Pleasant Winter reached forward and embraced him. "I knew these were important. It is good that you remember your old family and not just your new family here. We will have children if you wish; Gich Manidoo will bless us, and you can share these items with them."

Charles' body stiffened as she talked. He had never dared express his thoughts of escaping and returning to Massachusetts. It was his duty, but it seemed so far away.

Snow began to fall, large white flakes. They seemed to be purifying the earth as they lay down a soft white blanket upon all surfaces. Pleasant Winter could feel Charles' tension, and she pressed her body into his. She began to rub his neck and her other hand found his manhood. Charles jerked, but allowed her to continue. They began to take heavy breaths as their hearts began to race. Charles aroused, began to fondle her breasts. Her bronze body glistened in the yellow moonlight and her forbidden fruit became ready for harvest. Suddenly, wrapped up in the passion they could no longer feel the cold air. Charles' mouth found hers and the two rolled onto the hide, Charles upon her in bated lust. After several moments Pleasant Winter rolled Charles off her and she ripped open his shirt, smothering his chest and stomach with wet kisses.

Charles was suddenly taken back by his carnal passions but for untold reasons could not control himself. She pulled Charles up to his knees, and Pleasant Winter braced herself on all fours before him. Lifting her deerskin dress, she presented herself to his full manhood like a wild animal. Both allowed their unchecked passion and lust to spew forth, smoothing each other and engorging themselves with emotions and sexual fulfillment. Charles thrust forward. Pleasant Winter arched her back resembling a rutting stag and his craving doe. It was not long, and the two lustful bodies fell lifeless onto the bear hide, intertwining themselves in ecstasy.

In about an hour, Charles and Pleasant Winter awoke shivering in the frigid November night. She led him back to the warmth of the longhouse, and they slept there for the rest of the night. Charles had betrayed Mary, but at what cost. If he ever expected to escape he must assimilate. If only as a facade, he must do what ever it would take to get home to his family; it was another form of war. This time, his battlefield would be within.

ESCAPE

Just before dawn, Charles quietly slipped out from under the warm blankets and animal robe and left the longhouse. He went to the river and washed his face in the icy water, which immediately woke him. Then he walked to the fire pit closest to his longhouse and kindled the fire. Charles pulled his letter book from his shirt and taking a piece of charcoal from the fire pit, drew a group of stars in the shape of a bear representing the winter sky. Then he drew some stalks of maize and a single sunflower sticking out the center of them.

Tearing the page carefully from his book, Charles folded it and placed it in his shirt. Then he gathered his blanket and met the other hunters at the canoe. One of the village elders was standing with the two Indian hunters by the river. The elder motioned for Charles to join them.

The old man brought a shell up to his lips and blew on some coals within it until they glowed red. Then he added several herbs and grasses and began to chant. The mixture started to smolder, and he again blew into the shell. Lifting the shell above his head, the elder reverently closed his eyes and drew the smoke over himself with the motions of his hand. He then turned to the North, South, East and West and raised the shell to the sky each time. Finally, while chanting, the old Indian waved or smudged smoke over each of the three hunters as he passed the shell over each of their heads. All this was done to insure a successful hunt.

The three hunters, Charles, Waw-mawsh-kay-she (The Deer), and Pe-me-bot-tot (He That Runs) performed final checks on their gear and just as they were climbing into the canoe, Pleasant Winter appeared on the beach. She reached out and with a soft touch took Charles' hand.

"Be safe, my husband," she said softly.

Charles slid the folded piece of paper from his shirt into her hand as the canoe pulled away from shore and headed north. The canoe glided into the middle of the river, and Charles turned around and saw Pleasant Winter clutching the drawing to her breast. She knew its importance, being made from Charles' special book, with the writing for his children.

Within a few moments the two large islands of the river appeared, and the opening into the waterway the French called Lac St. Clair came into view. This lake, in good weather like this day, only took one day to paddle. By evening, the three had reached another river, and they pulled ashore, ate a cold meal and slept a few hours. Before dawn, they awoke and were traveling the river. By noon the river opened into a vast lake, one that you could not see from shore to shore. Lake of the Hurons, as it was called, proved to be much larger than Lake Erie, South of Pontchartrain.

From here Northward, the three men took turns paddling, hugging the Western shore. At first, hardwood stands of maples, elms and many oaks covered the woods. Periodically, these forests were broken by large oak openings, places where the majestic oaks towered high in a canopy over a very acidic soil nearly barren of undergrowth.

On the second day, large white pines began to intermix in the forest shore. On the third day, as they turned their canoe West and rounded a high peninsula, they entered a bay called Saginaw by the Indians. The bay alone was larger than Lake George.

A few miles into the bay, the men pulled their canoe into a marshy area on the Southern shore. The hunters concealed their canoe under weeds and brush. They marched inland about half a mile and set up a base camp. The men cut saplings and bent them into a frame and covered the frame with large pieces of bark they had brought. The floor of the hut was covered with several hides and in the center was placed a circle of rocks they collected for a fire pit. Once a fire was kindled, the men warmed gruel of wild rice and squirrel meat that they had packed along. It began to blow and an icy rain started to pelt the bark walls of their hut. The men were tired, and the cold weather mixed with the heat of the fire easily helped them drift to sleep.

Just before dawn, the hunters awoke and walked to the canoe. The Deer and Charles were going to take the canoe to the edge of the marsh and set up a hunting area where they hoped moose would cross. He Who Runs would travel West and look for signs of bear.

Charles got in the canoe, and he and The Deer pushed off into the water. It was slow going as they zigzagged around logs and diverted outcrops of land. The Deer had selected an area where a small rivulet flowed into the marsh with a small ravine that was opposite a modest knoll. The two men scouted the area for signs. Charles found some droppings that were fresh, and The Deer observed a well beaten down trail that was frequently used.

The Deer sat in a clump of hemlocks off the trail in the ravine. Charles sat about two rods behind him, concealed by a fallen log.

It wasn't long and snow began to fall. It was wet snow and the breeze was biting. Charles pulled the heavy blanket coat close around his neck and over his head. The two men remained very still.

The snow had accumulated about three inches in depth. Charles guessed that it was nearing twelve by the sun that peaked from the misty sky. The temperature was rising now, and snow began to melt and drip from the trees. Charles began to feel this would be an optimum time to attempt an escape. The dripping would conceal his movement.

Charles got on all fours and began to crawl on the ground toward The Deer. With the stealth of an animal, Charles moved several feet and then stopped, observed his prey and then resumed. Ever so slowly he inched on.

When Charles was about half way to The Deer, a blue jay released his caw of alarm. Charles froze, and he could see the Indian before him tense and reposition his musket. Should Charles rush forward or risk that he wouldn't be seen? He dared not move. Then meandering down the trail from the top of the knoll plodded a bull moose. Its movement had alerted the jay to movement in the forest. Unsuspectingly, the moose strolled down the trail; stopping to take nibbles of soft green foliage on his way. Cautiously, The Deer raised his musket to his shoulder. He was totally distracted by the moose. This would be a good day, and meat would be taken back to the tribe. Easing the cock of his musket back, The Deer took his final aim. Hisssssss – and with a deep cracking explosion the musket discharged. Instantly, the moose's head reared back, it took a single leap on all fours, let out a hideous snort and bellow, and fell crashing to the ground.

Charles jumped to his feet and grabbed an oak limb about four inches in diameter and ran towards The Deer. This was Charles' chance, the Indian was unaware of his presence, and his weapon was empty. Charles drew the oak club back with all his might, as if he would attempt to split a dense, gnarly, burled stump.

Hearing footsteps behind him The Deer turned about just in time to see the swing of the oak club before his face. Charles swung the limb bashing the Indian between the eyes, knocking him flat on his back. Charles immediately drew his knife to finish the Indian off. The Deer shook several times, his eyes rolled back in his head, and a trickle of blood oozed from his nose and mouth. He then became still, deadly still.

Charles took the Indian for dead and grabbed what he could in haste. He That Runs may have heard the musket shot and come to see if they had success. Charles slung the musket over his shoulder, put The Deer's bullet pouch and powder horn over the other shoulder and ran over to the moose. Charles knelt down and skillfully cut off a large strip of meat from the animal, placed it in his shirt, and turned one more time to look at the Indian still lifeless on the ground.

Charles sprinted to the top of the knoll and squatted on his haunches and scanned the area. Seeing nothing, he rushed to the canoe, unburied it and shoved off, leaving the bay as fast as he could paddle.

Charles' objective now was to survive detection by French allied natives and not perish in the fast approaching winter. With his canoe heading South, Charles skirted the Western shore of the Lake of the Hurons. The snow stopped and Charles pushed his canoe as fast as he could. He was continually vigilant, scanning the lake for other watercraft. When dusk arrived, he counted his blessings. There was little moon this evening. He had paddled nearly fifty miles, and he judged that it was a safe distance North of the villages around Fort Pontchartrain. Charles turned his canoe East and paddled straight across the tip of the lake. He was fully aware that he must bypass all French posts and Indian villages if possible. Charles paddled all night.

Daybreak found Charles pulling onto the Eastern shore of the lake. He must now travel overland if he was to avoid the fort and villages. Charles quickly knocked a hole in the bark canoe bottom and sank it in an endeavor not to leave evidence of his route. Scanning the West, he thought he caught the glimpse of movement on the lake. Charles couldn't be sure, but could not afford the time to linger on the beach. He shouldered his musket, accouterments and marched southeast toward where he hoped Lake of the Erie would be.

Charles was lucky for the next two days were warm, staying above freezing. He pushed himself and dared not stop to kindle fires. He was also lucky that it had not snowed again, and he could easily maneuver the several inches of sparse snow.

On the morning of the third day of his march, the sky was full of moisture. There were no clouds, but a sky full of white haze and mist. After several hours, the wind began to blow, and the temperature dropped.

Charles forded a river just as it began to snow again. The temperature dropped more, and thinking it safe, Charles made a quick shelter of pine bows by a large downed tree trunk. He scraped away the snow and kindled a fire. Charles knew he must warm himself and eat some warmed moose. As the storm began to rage, Charles ate a good portion of meat and dried the rest of the moose meat. Charles cut the meat into strips and laid them over a stick suspended over the fire, which he allowed to burn very low. He had to preserve the rest of the meat to keep him going. While he was waiting for the meat to dry, Charles made a rude form of snowshoes out of saplings and spruce root.

After several hours, Charles extinguished the fire, tied on the snowshoes he had made and headed southeast once again. He had warmed himself and had taken nourishment.

The snow continued until several hours after sunset. Charles continued, and when he judged it to be several hours before daylight, Charles deemed it time to stop. He found a stand of young pines about four feet tall. They were growing about an old stump. Charles rested his back against the stump and pulled his blanket coat over his head and fell asleep.

Charles woke slightly after sunrise. He stirred and shook his head. Snow slid off his woolen shroud. He could sense movement before him, but the young pines blocked his view. Charles slowly crawled to the edge of the trees and peered out. Before him was a deer carcass that was being gnawed on by a possum. Charles looked about him to make sure no other animals or humans were in sight. He picked up a stout branch. Charles jumped out of the trees yelling and ran toward the animal, which dropped to the ground and pretended it was dead. Charles swung the branch striking the possum. It rose quickly and swung its head toward Charles, showing its teeth like a mad dog and began to growl and bark. Charles continued striking at the animal and it lunged forward snapping at the branch with each motion. After a few moments, the possum realized Charles was not going to give up, and it scurried off into the forest.

Charles took his knife and quickly skinned the deer. He rolled the hide and tied it to the strap of his equipment. The meat was putrid, not suitable for him to eat, so Charles took his musket and gear moving off toward Lake of the Erie.

All day, Charles walked on watching the sun to keep his bearings. It was a long day's march but a few hours after sunset Charles had reached Lake of the Erie. He knew that his time would be limited as to how long he would have for water travel and that would be the key to getting home. The lake could freeze shut any day. There would not be time to build a bark canoe.

Charles cautiously walked East, skirting the coast of the lake. Shortly after sunrise the next day, Charles smelled smoke. He moved farther East with his eyes peeled for the French or their Indians. Rounding a small peninsula Charles spotted a winter hunting lodge. He took it to be that of a Huron family. The lodge was a matt covered hut. Behind the lodge Charles watched an Indian woman scraping hides, preparing them for making clothing. Charles sat and watched. By the lakeshore, just on the beach was a small bark canoe about a rod long. Charles knew there must be one or two Huron hunters nearby. Still no sign and he was desperate.

Charles stood and walked toward the canoe. He did not look at the lodge. He wanted to appear that he was another Indian hunting along the shore. Covered in old paint, dirt and clothed as a native he imagined he should have no problem deceiving them, if only temporarily. From the corner of his eye, Charles saw the woman stand upright from her work. She took several steps. A few more steps and Charles was at the canoe. He tossed his musket in the boat and shoved it into the lake, jumped in and began to paddle.

"Pa-kau, Mau-tchi au-ne-ne, Pa-kau! (Stop, bad man, stop)" yelled the woman. She continued yelling at Charles as she ran to the shore. Then up the lake a puff of smoke, the deep thud of a musket and Charles was knocked over in the canoe. His left arm stung like a dozen bee stings, and blood began to squirt from his bicep. He had been shot by an Indian returning to camp who had been alarmed by the woman yelling. Charles pulled himself back to his knees and paddled as best he could with one arm. He spun his head about to see the Indian reloading his musket. Charles pulled harder on the paddle. Thud! Splash, the ball fell short hitting the water just beside Charles. Within minutes, Charles had paddled himself out of range, and he slowed his pace. After another half hour Charles stopped paddling to see to his wound.

Charles tore open the sleeve of his blood soaked shirt. He pulled his knife and cut off a strip of linen from the bottom of the shirt and cringed as he put pressure on the wound. After a few moments, Charles dipped the cloth strip into the cold lake water and rinsed it out as much as he could. Then he looked over the wound. There did not seem to be any damage to the bone; the bullet had entered in the front of the arm and gone through the arm exiting on the back of the arm several inches below the shoulder. Wasting no more time, Charles rinsed off his arm again and wrapped the wet rag around his arm as a snug bandage. With the stolen canoe he continued on his Eastern journey.

For the next four days, Charles paddled on the big lake. Luck in the form of seasonable weather was with him for the ice did not form, and the snow was only minimal. Several times the winds blew, and at those times Charles landed his canoe and slept for a few hours. Every day Charles rinsed out the bandage and washed and saw to his wound.

On the fourth afternoon, the current of the lake told Charles he was approaching the mouth of the river that fed the lake. Charles turned his canoe South and crossed to avoid French posts and patrols. In what Charles estimated at less than ten miles, he reached the South shore of the lake. Here he hid the canoe. The worst of his journey would now begin. He must march overland due East in the hopes of reaching English settlements before he froze or starved to death.

Charles was determined and set off briskly walking East. He was not sure, but reckoned he would walk three to five weeks before arriving in English territory. Meanwhile, he must keep a watchful eye out for Indians and French. Much of Charles' supply of food had dwindled, and he attempted to ration out the remaining morsels. On the second day, he happened upon a wild berry patch. Feeling weakened from hunger, Charles filled his mouth full of the red treats. They were frozen, but still would allow some nourishment. He quickly picked several handfuls and put them in his shirt for later. Then Charles filled his mouth once more.

Suddenly, there was a crashing noise from the bushes to his right. Charles poised ready for anything. Out of the brush popped an angry growling black bear! Charles grabbed his musket in his left hand, cocked it, somehow brought it up to his shoulder and pulled the trigger. Snap! His musket misfired. Charles had no choice now but to turn around and run for his life. With the bear close at his heals, Charles scrambled to the top of a ridge. Suddenly, he could no longer hear the bear. Charles turned about and could not believe what he saw. The bear was stopped in the center of the berry patch gorging himself. Charles didn't wait and watch, he took off in case the bear changed its mind about pursuit.

By the next day, Charles' arm was very sore, and he was quite weak again. The snow had begun to fall the night before, and his travel was slowing now. Late in the day, Charles crossed a river and stopped, hoping to catch some fish. He made a spear by sharpening the end of a stick, but had no luck. Finally, just before dark, Charles found a small pool formed by a bend in the river. In the pool Charles could see some minnows. He took some bark from a tree and using it like a scoop collected about two dozen that he ate on the spot.

By late afternoon the next day, the terrain was changing. Rolling hills stood before him, and the forest became thicker. Just before sunset a lake appeared to the South. Charles knew this could mean settlements, but he had not traveled far enough East to be out of Indian territory. Charles could only continue, but he was now severely malnutritioned, and his arm was swollen and oozing yellow puss.

The next morning, Charles saw another lake and just before dark another. Now he thought he knew where he was. The Ottawa had told of the lakes to the East, an area where the Iroquois live, where tribes of the Seneca, Oneida, Onondaga, Cayuga and Tuscaroras have their villages. Just East of these lakes, settled in a quaint valley, is the land of the Mohawks and the Mohawk River. If he would make it there, he would find friendly help.

Now nearing the end of January, the weather was becoming unbearable. This morning, Charles knew a storm was on its way. He could see it in the sky and feel it in the wind. He had to find food if he was to continue. The only sure way was to head Southeast and hope to arrive at the Iroquois lakes. There, if he was unnoticed, he could find food.

That afternoon, Charles crested a hill and saw a lake in the valley below. Charles carefully walked down the hill to the lake. Pausing on the edge of the woods, Charles scanned the partially frozen lake for movement. He chopped a hole in the ice close to the shore with his belt axe and waited for fish to swim under. He had made another spear. After several hours, Charles had not had any luck. Then he saw movement and jumped up to run to the woods. He had spotted Indians on the opposite shore. The ice under him was too thin and had been weakened by chopping the hole. Crack, then a creaking sound, Charles froze. Splash, he went through the ice. Charles was lucky the water was only knee deep and he quickly pulled himself out and made a beeline for the trees. Charles hid for about an hour.

Charles could smell smoke in the wind, so he began to walk in the direction from which it blew. His legs now ached from the dunking in the frozen lake. He continued on in pain. The lay of the land was quite rocky, full of shale, and the icy rock croppings were dangerous. About a mile distance, Charles could see smoke. He moved ever so slowly now, not wanting to be discovered. From the edge of a clearing, Charles spotted a village and to his right the scant leftovers of a field of maize. Charles carefully made his way to the field crawling and rooting in the snow for leftover ears or kernels from the tribe's harvest. He found enough to make several meals and slowly backed out into the woods.

At this point, Charles could feel much more pain in his body. His arm ached, his feet had stinging pain and his stomach had a continual dull suffering. The weather also was closing in on him as snow began to fall and the wind picked up. It felt and looked like a blizzard. Charles had to find shelter. He put a hand full of corn in his mouth and marched East, attempting to put distance between himself and the Indians. Charles forced himself to continue on for nearly two hours.

It was becoming dusk and the snow was piling up. Charles was maneuvering around an outcrop at the edge of a small gorge, and before him was his salvation, the opening of a small cave. Charles crawled in the opening, which immediately turned to the right. He backed out and collected some sticks and wood, he had to have a fire quickly. The storm was now a full-blown blizzard.

Charles again entered the cave. He took a small amount of dried cedar bark he peeled from an old dead fall and formed it into the shape of a bird's nest. Then he took the flint from his musket and began striking it against his knife. The sparks this created fell into a piece of char-cloth from his haversack and caused the char-cloth to glow red. Charles took the char-cloth and put it in the bird's nest and held it above his head and blew steadily into it. Smoke spewed from it. In no time it burst into flames and Charles quickly placed the nest on the floor of the cave and began to place sticks about the flame until he had a warm blaze going.

Charles had to see to his other immediate needs now. He placed the blade of his knife in the fire and began to take off wet clothing, his moccasins, leggings, and his blanket coat. Charles, in an effort to dry them, braced most of these against the walls of the cave with sticks. Then Charles sat as close to the fire as he could tolerate and rubbed his feet and legs vigorously. He was lucky they were not frostbitten.

When he started to feel some sensation coming back, Charles ate some of the corn and drank water from his canteen. For over an hour he sat there and rotated his clothing so they dried and continued to eat corn and warm himself.

There was one last thing he must do in order to see to his well being. His arm had been festering, and it had begun oozing. The early stages of gangrene were taking hold. Charles took off his shirt and found a semi-clean spot of fabric and tore it off the shirt. Then he laid the warmed coat on the ground by the fire, sat on it as a robe and fed the fire once again. Now Charles placed a stick between his jaws and bit down. He sprinkled gunpowder from the powder horn into the wound. Taking his knife from the fire and without hesitation held the knife's glowing red tip to his arm. The wound sizzled and smoked as the powder and flesh blended to cauterize it. Charles bit down on the stick as every muscle in his body clinched. He dropped the knife, and slumped over onto the coat passed out.

Charles opened his eyes. It was very dark in the cave, and he was cold but wrapped in his blanket coat. Charles lay there for a short time gaining his composure. After a while, he rolled over and lit a new fire as he had before. The coals left in the fire pit were as cold as he. After warming himself, Charles took some corn and a sip of water from his canteen.

As the fire dwindled, Charles, still weak, crawled to the front of the cave. The snow had fallen so deep that he had to dig his way out; it was now over three feet deep and still coming down. Charles guessed he had slept on and off for several days.

He inspected his shoulder. There was quite a scar but at least it was not oozing or bleeding any longer. If he was to make it back home, he knew he only had several days of strength left in him.

Charles put on all the clothes and tied on his snowshoes. He crawled out the cave and took a few steps. He was shaky on his feet. Charles rooted around and found a stout stick to use as a walking stick and began to move East. He believed that he must now march until he dropped in his own tracks if he was to succeed. He marched on, limping and staggering, trudging onward for four days and three long nights. He stopped at rivers and drank or ate snow for water. He lived on a half a handful of corn or weeds he rooted from under the snow daily.

On the fourth day, shortly after the sun reached its zenith, Charles stopped for a short rest; he was now on his last leg and doubted if he would make it through the night. Behind him he saw movement, at the crest of the knoll that he had just passed, about quarter a mile back. It was a man, appearing to be an Indian sneaking from tree to tree, tracking Charles. Had someone been following him the entire way?

Charles jumped to his feet and with every ounce of strength left he began to jog forward up and over another knoll. Just as he crested the top, Charles stumbled and fell rolling and tumbling down the hill toward a river below. He struggled to his feet. He was now exhausted. It took every effort to carry his musket, but he staggered on toward the river like a wounded deer taking a step here and a step there, changing directions, all hunched over, barely able to breath. Suddenly, Charles collapsed and fell on his side then rolling onto his back. Charles stared into the sky; his vision was blurry as he tried to catch his breath, wheezing and hacking. His stomach was empty; he had no more energy; his lungs and throat burned.

From the water's edge, Charles could see a man approaching, a white man dressed in a long greatcoat and tricorn hat tied to his head by a woolen scarf. He consciously stepped toward Charles. The man reached out with his long Dutch style fowler and nudged Charles in the ribs. Charles flinched and gasped, and the man jumped.

"I thought ye was a Red Indian! Yur a white man," exclaimed the man in a heavy German/Dutch accent. "Whut happen da ya?"

Charles moaned. "Help me," was all he could get out in a wheezing, rasping whisper.

"Wait ear, I'll be a right bauk," said the man urgently.

It wasn't long, and he returned with a toboggan. He rolled Charles onto the sled, and tied Charles to it so he didn't fall off.

"I'm Nicholas Herkimer. I has a ferm oder der." Herkimer pointed southeast. "Hoed on we get da der for dum help."

Charles looked as bad as he felt. His clothing was Indian fashion. They were torn, many in shreds and stained with filth, dirt and dried blood. His arms and legs were scratched and cut. His face was covered by dirt and blood. Charles' hair had grown out several inches but was all matted to his head. His body and face were gaunt.

Herkimer threw the toboggan rope over his shoulder and pulled Charles to his farm. He took Charles to his house, which was a modest frontier log cabin. Putting Charles' arm around his head, Herkimer struggled getting Charles inside. The door flew open and the two stepped in. Herkimer managed to get Charles on his bed, and Charles passed out of exhaustion.

It wasn't long and the talking of Herkimer and another man woke Charles. They were discussing Charles' condition. The room was very warm. There was a great blaze in the fireplace. The other man dipped some broth from a kettle by the fire and took it to Charles.

"Ear da go. Ya dink dis young man," urged the man. "Dis good broth. Ear's some bread da go wit it."

Charles took the broth and bread and began to eat.

"I is Johan Herkimer. I is Nicholas' fadder. Ya will feel bedder after ya eats. Where ya come from?" Asked Johan.

Charles dipped the bread into the steaming broth. "It's been a long journey. I was taken captive when the French and Indians attacked Fort William Henry. The Ottawa took me back to their tribe and adopted me. I was able to make my escape." Charles took another large bite of bread and slurped up some broth. "Where are we? Is this New York?" Asked Charles.

"Ya dis tis New York. Dis is ya Mohawk Valley, and we's not too far from Albany. Ya rest and in couple days I send you ta

Fort Johnson wit my son Henry," replied Johan. "Eats and sleep. Make ya stronger."

Charles ate his fill, and Nicholas saw to cleaning and dressing Charles' wounds. After two days, Charles became quite insistent on being transported East. Nicholas gave Charles a woolen set of clothes and he dressed quickly. Nicholas and Henry Herkimer put Charles on a sleigh and wrapped him in animal robes. Nicholas and his father bid Charles farewell, and Henry drove the sleigh East along the edge of the Mohawk River.

It was a crisp, cold morning. Frost covered everything, and steam billowed from the horse's nostrils as they plodded forward. The valley was very peaceful, and as they progressed Charles dozed on and off. There were not many homes along the route but those that were, appeared modest frontier homes. Charles was impressed at how many were nestled in the hilltops above the valley. Many of these farms had square one-story barns. The barn roofs were very steeply pitched, and they were built with wagon doors on both ends with narrow clapboard walls.

Toward the end of the day, the sleigh crossed the river and pulled to a stone house near the river's edge. Outside there were several Mohawk Indians and English traders. They apparently were negotiating a deal around a fire. One of the men stepped up to the house's entrance as the sleigh approached. From the door stepped a man Charles knew, General Johnson. Johnson motioned for several men to lend a hand with Charles.

"Nurse, where ye hell ya been? Are ye lame or have ya been fighten a bear?" asked Johnson in his Irish brogue. He walked to Charles and helped lead him into the house.

"I was one of those captured at Fort William Henry this summer. The Ottawa took me to their lands in the West, but I saw my chance and escaped. I'd be much obliged for a night's rest and help getting back East," explained Charles.

"That battle has affected many more of us than was reckoned. I'd heard about ye battle, and me and many of my brothers ye Mohawks and me agents rushed to Fort Edward, but we could not get General Webb to march to your relief. We met in his quarters at Fort Edward, me and my men, all dressed in Indian fashion, white and Indian alike, ready to battle. We were disgusted with him. I reached down and pulled off my right leggin and threw it to the ground before the General. 'Will ye lead us to relieve Fort William Henry?' I urged.

"'No, sir. We will not be sending relief from here,' had been Webb's answer. So the entire party with me pulled off their right leggin and threw them before Webb.

"'Will ye allow us to march to the relief of Fort William Henry?' I asked in a commanding tone.

"'I refuse,' stated Webb.

"I pulled off the other leggin and threw it to the pile, and my men did the same.

"'Will ye let us go to Fort William Henry,' I yelled.

"'I order you not to leave this fort,' arrogantly retorted Webb.

"All the whites and Indians alike in my party stripped off all our clothing excepting our breechcloth and threw them in a great pile in from of the General making sure he understood our great distaste for he now ordering us to stay put. Me Irish temper had now hit a boiling. I turned to the leaders of my militia of Mohawks and Whites and nodded. Webb looked as if he was about to say more. I drew my belt axe from my sash, as did all my comrades and we lifted them above our heads and bellowed a loud, intimidating war hoop. Webb cringed and dared not say a word. All of us threw our axes in the corner of the room and stormed out in disgust." Johnson's face was flushed with anger recounting the incident.

He continued. "I and me agents are still negotiating for the release of some of the prisoners from the battle.

"My brothers, ye Mohawks were telling me ye Algonquians had some prisoners far to the West, near Fort Ponchartrain. Looks like you've had ye hard march. Come and take a wee brandy with me, and me wife Molly will fix ya a feast," boasted Johnson.

"I'd be honored General," replied Charles.

The two men, along with Henry Herkimer and two of Johnson's agents spent a short but pleasant evening of food and drink. Charles was feeling very relieved at being back amongst fellow Englishmen.

"You have a lovely home General," admired Charles.

"I have worked hard at making it a proper home even though it be here in the wilderness," said Johnson with pride.

"I was wondering sir, why it is called Fort Johnson? Henry and several others have called it so," asked Charles.

"It is a place of retreat, a place when we could make a stand if need be. It is a stout house with overhangs in the attic. If needed, we can open firing doors from the attic and shoot down on ye enemy. I also have ordered masons to chisel gun loops in the basement walls. Eye, if need be we can muster ye militia and Mohawks near by and hold up here," explained the General.

The next morning, refreshed, Charles was treated to a fine meal of bread pudding, Dutch sausages and steaming tea.

"I have asked Mr. Wraxall to accompany ya East," offered Johnson. "Where are ya heading for? I hear Rogers is formed another company, a company of volunteers to learn ye scouten and rangen. I also hear that he's a leaden an expedition North from Fort Edward and looken for more men."

"To be totally honest, I survived the past months with the thoughts of making it back to home, to my wife and my family. She was with child, and we should have a son or daughter by now. I am at a loss though on heading directly there. I, like you, have experienced some of the native life. I have seen and witnessed things different than other New Englanders. I've also done things I am not proud of. Things that I do not dare tell. Things that may destroy the life I once had," explained Charles sincerely.

"Eye, tis a different life than ours, but a good life for their beliefs. You'll forever be haunted by your experiences in this war, and you'll be always knowing in ye own mind what ya done. Ya may need some time. Eye, some time before ye return to ye family and civilization. It may do ye some good to go via Fort Edward, then home," reasoned Johnson.

"I believe you speak with great wisdom, sir. But I must get word to my family that I am safe and will be returning," said Charles.

"Eye, ya write a letter and I'll dispatch it to ye family. Mr. Wraxall will take ya to Fort Edward. From there ya can make peace with yourself and find your way home from there," insisted Johnson.

Charles sat at the desk in the corner of the room and began a letter to Mary.

My Dearest Mary,

I have finally arrived back at civilization and the English Colonies. By now you have probably thought me dead. I am sure you have heard of the great battle and siege at Fort William Henry this past August. The enemy enveloped our fort, and we were forced to surrender. I will save the details for later.

After we surrendered, I sent you a letter via a scout the eve of our march, but alas, we were attacked by the enemy's savages and doubt if you received it. I was taken captive, and the Indians who took others and me escorted us back to their village at a place in the West, deep in French territory.

They adopted us into their tribe and though we suffered a great deal, we had little ill treatment. We were assimilated into families and were instructed in their ways.

Eventually, seeing my chance, I made my escape. I've been making my way East for quite some time now. I wait the day I can hold you again with great anxiety.

I have experienced unspeakable things. This is all I can say.

I must hurry now. I am being taken toward Fort Edward and must not tally any longer.

I have not asked, but am most exceedingly hopeful that you have delivered our child several months ago. I pray it went well for you and look forward to meeting my son or daughter. Give them a kiss from their father. Please tell mother and father I am safe now and will be home soon.

Yours Affectionately,
Charles

Charles and Peter Wraxall piled into the sleigh and bid farewell to General Johnson. The sleigh headed East by northeast. They held their course for nearly ten miles. Then they had left the Mohawk Valley and turned the sleigh northeast. The two men were following an old Indian trail that had been expanded into a passable wagon road. After about a dozen more miles they came to a river.

"We're close now, Nurse. This is the Hudson," explained Wraxall.

They followed the river East for only several miles. The land now was very common for Charles; he had marched it often. They were on the military road that leads between Fort Edward and Lake George. The men headed southeast.

The sleigh rounded a bend, and six woolen clad men stepped into the road. Wraxall reined in the horse.

"Halt," yelled out one of the men. "Who are ye?"

"Peter Wraxall, secretary to General Johnson of New York and Charles Nurse, sergeant of Massachusetts colony," replied Wraxall.

"What's your business?" asked the guard.

"I'm escorting Sergeant Nurse. He was taken prisoner at the siege of Fort William Henry and escaped and is returning to duty here at Fort Edward," stated Wraxall.

"Very well, you may pass. Report to ye fort commander," ordered the guard.

Wraxall skid the sleigh over the Hudson River and onto the road before the fort, stopping at the West gate. Charles was escorted into the commandant's office in the fort. Entering the room, Charles snapped to attention and saluted.

"Sir, Sergeant Charles Nurse, Massachusetts Bay, reporting for duty," respectfully stated Charles.

"Your regiments are long gone from here for home sergeant," replied Lt. Colonel Haviland.

"Yes sir. I was captured at the siege and was taken to Indian territory in the West. I escaped and have arrived again to redeem myself, sir," clearly stated Charles.

The Lt. Colonel looked up at Charles, cocked his head and continued. "A little worse for the wear aren't you, Sergeant? Are you fit for duty?"

"Sir, with a few days recuperation I will be," answered Charles.

"What duty are you volunteering for then?" asked Haviland. "Your Massachusetts men are gone."

"I have served with Captain Rogers before, and I hear he is preparing to march. I'd like to accompany him once again, if you wish, sir," replied Charles confidently.

"He is under my command," Haviland said slightly arrogantly. "I believe we can find you quarters to rest a few days on the Great Island. Report to the surgeon at the main hospital building and then on Wednesday report to Major Rogers. If he'll have you, I'll write you orders to join him," ordered Haviland.

Charles left the commandant's quarters and walked West over the bridge from the fort to the Great Island. Things had changed. The bridge was made of bateaux tied together with a large cable and covered with wood planks. There was a guardhouse at each end of the bridge. Charles turned left once on the island. He followed the path in the snow leading to the South. On his left was a rear guard shack. On his right there were many, many houses, shacks and huts. These structures were quite regular, laid out similar to a tent encampment. There were officers' houses arranged in pyramid shape with commanders at the peak and subalterns at the base. Rows of enlisted men's huts were in straight regular streets. Beyond these huts, Charles could see a large parade ground and another guard area. Farther South Charles passed storehouses, a blockhouse and hospital buildings.

Charles reported to the main hospital where a surgeon cleaned and dressed his wounds and addressed his symptoms. The surgeon prescribed a tincture of rhubarb daily, a healthy issue of rum for a week and a diet of greens. He suspected Charles was suffering from scurvy. The surgeon had Charles quartered in the blockhouse.

For almost a week, Charles stayed close to the blockhouse where a surgeon's mate attended several sick men housed with him. Once a day, Charles would walk the wharf area northeast of the blockhouse. Here Charles relaxed, watching the guards and the movement around the fort and surrounding area.

REDEMPTION

By March, Charles felt he had recuperated enough and chose to report to Captain Rogers. Charles left the blockhouse and marched toward the area of the officers' huts. He was confident and swaggered slightly as he marched.

As Charles approached Rogers' house two guards before the door stopped him. "Halt there, who are ye and what's yer business with the Captain," questioned the guard.

"I am Sergeant Charles Nurse of the Massachusetts-Bay Colony. I have been ordered by Colonel Haviland to report to the Captain for duty," replied Charles as he handed his papers to the guard.

"Looks like ye Colonel's signature. You just wait here," ordered the guard, who turned about, knocked on the door and entered the house.

Charles turned his back to the house and adjusted his coat and pulled his scarf closer about his neck. Three men left an officer's hut to the left, and the trio marched toward Charles. Two of the men were six feet or near, and the third was lucky if he were five foot seven. Their strides were purposeful as they walked directly toward Rogers' house. As they approached Charles could see silver gorgets around each man's neck. Charles quit fumbling with his clothes and snapped a salute. The three men halted just before Charles. All four men were taken back with a loss of words for a moment.

"Jesus Christ, if it isn't Nurse," shouted the officer on the right. "Haven't seen nor heard of you in some time now," continued Burbank.

"What makes ye think you can loiter here in front of ye Captain's house, soldier?" scoffed McCurdy.

"Sergeant, we heard you were dead. Heard the Injuns took you after the massacre at Fort William Henry," said Moore as he stuck out his hand to shake Charles'.

"Relax Nurse, yer amongst friends," laughed Moore.

"Yes sir, I mean yes Increase, I mean, yes lieutenant," stammered Charles.

"Put your arm down Nurse. God sake we've been through some times together," encouraged Moore.

The four men patted each other on the back and greeted each other with warm handshakes.

"I remember when you were sergeants and I was a corporal. Remember when we hauled those boats over that damned mountain?" Charles joked.

"Eye, it was great times, and we really put the sneak on those Frenchies," offered McCurdy.

"So what ya here for Nurse, trying to get back with us for another push North? Ya know all yer brothers of the Bay are marched home?" asked Burbank.

Charles' face changed. His brow narrowed and his eyes squinted, his mouth frowned and he lowered his head slightly. "I have some business to settle," sternly stated Charles. "You are correct Lieutenant that I was taken by the Indians after the massacre. I saw many men butchered. I saw men eaten by the savages. I was stripped naked and forced to be one of the red fiends. I was made to do things unspeakable, but I intend on taking redemption for the actions of those hellhounds!"

The three officers understood and spoke few words. "Come in with us Nurse; we have some business with the Captain as well," said Lieutenant Moore as he put his hand on Charles' shoulder and lead him in the front door of the house.

The door opened, and the four walked in. Seated at a desk was a clerk taking notes, and pacing back and forth was Robert Rogers. He was as Charles remembered him but slightly worn for the wear. The four men saluted the Captain, who returned the salute without looking at them.

He continued his dictation. "Colonel, I fully understand it is your prerogative to send forth what details and scouts you wish, and I would never disobey your orders for such. I have for some time now offered to lead a sizable detachment against our enemies to the North and capture the garrisons at Ticonderoga and St. Frederic. I believe that this can be done without much opposition during the winter. I appreciate your intent and the orders you have issued me to march forth with a 400-man force for that purpose. The only concern, sir, is that you have chosen to make these orders public. You have stated that upon Putnam's return of his scout that I am to march North. Now if any spy is amongst us, or if a man deserts or is captured, the enemy, as well, may be in waiting. I, sir, am your most humble and obedient servant, etc., etc."

The four men took off there greatcoats. Charles was impressed. Burbank, McCurdy and Moore were all dressed in like uniforms. Rogers, as well, was dressed similarly. It was apparent that Rogers had now uniformed his rangers. They were dressed in green regimental coats and waistcoats. The coarse wool was heavy, suitable for the cold of winter. Rogers also had gone a step further and dawned matching breeches. The coats and waistcoats had pewter buttons, and their regimental coats were laced in silver braid.

Rogers now turned to the four men and stood at attention, stretching himself to his full impressive height.

"Gentlemen," greeted Rogers.

The four saluted, and Captain Rogers returned the salute.

"Captain, we have seen to the preparations, and the men are finalizing the work on the snow shoes. Each man is to have a pair plus skates, and every dozen is to have a hand sleigh to pull. The rations and powder have been requested from the commissary at the fort. I believe we are ready," reported Lieutenant Moore.

"We have several volunteers also, sir, of the twenty-seventh Regiment," read Lieutenant Burbank. "Captain Henry Pringle, Lieutenant Boyle Roche and the rest of the detachment of volunteers include an ensign, sergeant and one private. We also have Mr. Creed, Kent and Wrightson as other volunteers."

"It seems, Captain, that we've another volunteer; you remember Nurse, don't ya?" questioned Lieutenant McCurdy.

"Reporting for duty, Captain Rogers. I'd like to volunteer for your attack on the French. If you'll accept me," responded Charles.

Rogers strolled over to an armchair by the desk. He rubbed his chin and shuffled a few papers. Then he picked up the pile and tossed them in a pile.

"Damned paperwork. I'm a fighten soldier not a damned clerk," spouted Rogers. "Nurse, I had heard about your capture by the Indians, and that you had made your escape. Until I got the papers from Colonel Haviland I had no idea you'd be marching home via Fort Edward." Rogers paused. "So what is your reason for joining us as a volunteer?"

"You know me, and know that when given a duty, I always follow through, sir. I want dearly to be at home with my family, but as you know, things happen in war that changes you. There are things that I have seen, and things that happened in the past few months that I must deal with before returning home. I feel that if I go with you on this attack that I will be part of something that may set things straight."

Rogers got up and walked over to some coats hanging on pegs on the wall. He took down a greatcoat and put it on, and then he took a silver laced tricorn from another peg. He turned to Charles and spoke. "A good soldier you are, sergeant, and a good volunteer you'll be. If you are willing and physically able to accompany us on this march then I will have you with us. Report to the commissary for proper outfitting, see Ensign Joseph Waite for last minute directions, you'll be assigned to him, and be ready to march within the week," directed Rogers. "Welcome aboard Nurse," said Rogers, and he shook Charles' hand.

"Thank you, sir," replied Charles.

Rogers put on the hat, and the three lieutenants and he marched out. Charles left, as well, and reported as ordered.

On the morning of March 10, Charles awoke and dressed for the winter march to the French forts. Like many of the others, he wore woolen hose, breeches, waistcoat, a shirt and a coarse-heavy coat. Over this Charles wore a dark gray woolen greatcoat. He also had taken a tricorn and cut it down and tied it to his head with a warm scarf. Charles wrapped his feet in wool and wore a heavy pair of moccasins. Lastly, he put on a heavy pair of wool mittens and cut a hole in the right mitten so he could slide his fingers out to fire and load his musket.

Charles had been issued a Brown Bess musket from King's stores along with a powder horn and cartridge box, which he wore over his left shoulder and under his right arm. Under the other arm Charles slung a haversack full of food and a canteen full of water mixed with rum. Charles slung a hair-on knapsack over his back and across his shoulders like an Indian tumpline and with his snowshoes over his shoulder he formed in the line with the other rangers.

The men were awaiting orders, and Ensign Waite walked over and ordered, "Clarke and Nurse, see to the men of our company. I'll be getten final orders from the Captain."

"Eye, sir," replied Sergeant Clarke.

Charles and James Clarke walked up and down the line of men looking them over to make sure they were ready. Captain Rogers, Captain Bulkley, Lieutenants Crofton and Moore and Captain Pringle walked out of Rogers' quarters and marched to where the other officers were waiting. Charles and Clarke were within earshot.

"Are we all here, Pottinger, Campbell, Philips, Waite, McDonald, White, Ross?" listed Rogers as he counted heads. "All right, we have new orders which I am sure you all have heard by now. Our good Colonel has seen fit to send us off with 180 rather than 400. I have also been made aware that not only was Mr. Best's servant taken prisoner by an enemy party, Captain Putnam has informed me that one of his men deserted from a scout and that he believes that 600 Indians are not far from Ticonderoga. I do not understand why our numbers have been cut rather than increased, but our duty is not to question but rather follow orders." Rogers' motions were rather quick, and his mind seemed to be moving a mile a minute. "Damn it, we can still do this. If your men are prepared we have a well-trained force, and we have the advantage of a winter campaign. Let's march," ordered Rogers.

"Form for march," bellowed Rogers. "Follow me."

Rogers immediately marched over the bridge from the island to the mainland and turned North onto the road leading toward Lake George. The rest of the detachment followed six abreast with officers and sergeants spaced between squads. Once they left the security of the outer guards of the fort, Rogers gave orders.

"Crofton, take your men and form point, Moore form a rear guard, Pottinger take my right, and Philips you take the left."

Crofton and his men ran forward to secure the road. The rest of the men instinctively took their positions dropping their musket to their sides and took off on a slow jog moving along the road. It was a clear day, and the men made good time. Just before dusk Crofton came back to the main body and reported to Rogers that his advanced guard had arrived at Halfway Brook, and the area was safe from enemy. Rogers moved the entire detachment into an old stockade, posted guard and a roving guard, fed his men, and ordered all to get what rest they could.

On the eleventh, the detachment rose early and continued their march. By midmorning, they made it to the clearing where

Fort William Henry had stood. Just as they breeched the perimeter of trees, Charles stopped and stared. Before him stood the charred remnants of the fort and entrenched camp with blackened timbers peaking out of the white snow making a vivid contrast. In Charles' mind, he could see the smoke and flashes of the cannons from both the British and French; he could hear the yelling of orders and the men darting from one station to another. He was stricken with terror as he watched the massacre replay in his head: the men running, the Indians pulling men from formation and hacking at them, the men and women screaming and blood everywhere. He could see the savages holding their trophies above their heads, screaming with delight, a lone Indian coming out of the fort's casements thrusting a severed head oozing streams of blood into soldier's faces.

Sergeant Clarke jostled Charles back to consciousness, then they continued past the fort ruins and down to the water's edge. Here, Rogers gave orders for the men to tie on their skates. Now they would proceed by ice northward on Lake George. They glided single file along the west coastline of the ice. By dusk, they made it to the first set of narrows. Rogers gave orders for the detachment to camp on the East side of the lake. Parties were kept on guard all night, and a walking picket was also maintained. It snowed all night. A night scout was sent down the lake, but returned before daybreak having seen no sign of the enemy.

On the morning of the twelfth, Rogers had the men up and moving before daybreak, skating down the lake. At about three miles distance, Rogers, who was leading the column, halted the detachment. He called for Sergeant James Tute to move forward with a squad. Rogers had spied a dog on the ice and thought that could mean the enemy Indians may be laying in ambush, since it was common for there to be dogs with them. Rogers ordered everyone else to shore. Tute returned with no sign of the enemy.

Rogers held council with his officers and decided that they would proceed by land on snowshoes, so an enemy party on top of the surrounding hills could not see them. Snow began to fall again and periodically fell heavily. They made it to Sabbath Day Point, and Rogers ordered a rest. He also sent out several parties down the lake with telescopes to look for the enemy. At dusk, the scouts had found nothing, so Rogers pushed the detachment forward. Lieutenant Philips, with fifteen men on skates, was the advanced guard. Ensign Ross and a squad acted as the left flank while the rest of the party, led by Rogers, continued the march along the shore on snowshoes, single file, very close together, as the night being black as pitch.

Near eight miles from the enemy, advanced guard position Philips sent back a man on skates telling Rogers to halt the column. Rogers had everyone sit on the ice. Minutes later, Philips himself came back to Rogers and told him he had seen what he thought was a campfire on the Eastern shore. Rogers sent Philips and Ensign White to scout where he had seen the fire. In an hour, they returned convinced there was an enemy camp there.

Rogers called in the guards and ordered the men to prepare to attack the camp. They all stashed the sleighs and packs in a thicket, left a small guard with them and followed Rogers across the lake, moving in a single rank. Once close, Captain Rogers, Lieutenant Philips, Ensign White and twenty men began to crawl toward the site of the fire. The rest of the men continued slowly behind them. Rogers held up his hand to halt. Everyone stopped and lay on the ice. He and the advanced detachment continued slowly, but within a half hour returned finding nothing. Most expected that Philips had seen a mirage of sorts in the form of rotten wood or patches of snow, that at a distance can glow and resemble a fire. The men returned to the West shore and spent the rest of the night cold and shaking.

Just before the sun rose, Rogers called the officers together. It was decided to advance on snowshoes rather than risk being seen on the ice. Then the sergeants were called in.

Rogers gave his orders. "This is the spot we will set as our rendezvous if we need one. Hide the sleighs and extra equipment and provisions in that thicket," he pointed at the hiding spot. "Cunningham and Scott, you're staying with the packs. Have the men carry all their ammunition and three days of food and water. We are going to skirt the backside of these mountains. As you can see, it's snowing hard again, and the snow is nearly four feet deep. I want to make it to a spot between the advanced guard and the fort; that way, tonight we can lay ambush some enemy roads and apprehend them in the morning as they are switching their guards. We are going to advance in two divisions, Indian fashion, so we can pack the snow as we advance, making it better for each man as we move. I'll lead one, and Bulkley, you the other. Ensigns White and

Waite, you lead the rear guard. Ensign McDonald, you have the advanced guard. The rest of you should be spread out in your divisions. These divisions should march close to the base of the mountains, so there will be a natural barrier covering our right. We will keep the small creek on our left. If the enemy is moving, they will be taking the frozen creek bed as a road. Get ready to march."

In this manner, the detachment began on the thirteenth. They trudged forward on snowshoes until noon, and then Rogers called a halt. They were within two miles of the French advanced guard. Here they ate and drank a cold meal and checked their weapons. Rogers ordered the men to rest and wait until late afternoon in order to miss the movement of the afternoon enemy guard change.

At three o'clock, Rogers roused his men, and they began their march again. They made about one and a half miles, when a man came back from the advanced guard to report to Rogers that the enemy had been sighted. Almost immediately, another runner came back to Rogers.

"Captain, Ensign McDonald has counted ninety-six in the enemy party, and most of them are Indians. He said to tell you they are using the frozen river as you guessed."

"Go back up and tell McDonald to face his men all left and form my right flank and wait my gunfire to attack."

The man rushed back. Rogers gave orders to several runners to send the same message down the line, that the entire detachment was to face left, Ensigns White and Waite were to form his left flank, the entire detachment were to drop packs and advance to a few yards of the river bank. They were to extend the line along the bank, so the entire enemy party would be hit at the same time. Orders were to hold fire till Rogers fired first as a signal to attack with a volley.

Charles was several men left of Rogers as they took up positions. Many men hid behind trees or crouched behind the bank, which was high enough above the river to conceal them. The men waited, trying not to breath, not to move, not to give away their position.

Below them, the rangers watched as the painted devils glided single file along the icy river, many of them bent over, skulking like wild beasts as they moved forward. The enemy was mixed periodically with a few Frenchman as well. Moments passed, and the enemy's front crossed that area where Ensigns White and Waite hid. Charles saw Rogers slowly lift his musket to his shoulder. Charles knew it was time, so he selected a tall savage several yards to his left and took careful aim.

Rogers' musket roared and the entire bank of the river erupted as the rangers unleashed a massed volley into the side of the unsuspecting enemy. Several dozens of the enemy were killed instantly, and others fell or dropped to the ground, either wounded or attempting to dodge another volley. The Indians left standing returned fire and attempted to dash back from where they came. Rogers yelled for McDonald to stop the retreat of any enemy coming his way. McDonald and his party took off after the rear section of the enemy who were attempting to run.

Lunging forward after the volley, about half of Rogers' force jumped over the bank and charged the enemy on the ice. Charles was with this group determined to make sure that the ambush was total.

Emotions out of control now, Charles made it to the ice bounding and sliding with his musket in one hand and a cutlass in the other. When he hit the ice, he slashed one Indian in the gut, pulled up his musket and shot it into a Frenchman's head at point blank range, blood and brains spraying everywhere. Seeing an Indian attempting to crawl off the ice and up the bank, Charles dropped his musket and cutlass, jumped on the man as he pulled his scalping knife and slammed his knee into the Indian's back. Charles pulled up on the savage's hair with one hand and swung the knife with the other ripping and cutting the scalp from the enemy. Charles then pulled his belt axe and began to bash and hack two Indians who were wounded beside him. The one man curled up in a ball, attempting to cover himself against Charles' blows, but the other man lay lifeless after Charles' first swing of the axe.

At this time, the sound of many muskets toward McDonald's party snapped Charles' attention to his left. As he hesitated and listened, he saw Captain Rogers dispatch an Indian, who was obviously a war chief, with his axe and lift his scalp with one slash. Rogers dropped the Indian into the snow and stuffed the scalp into the bulging pocket of his coat.

"Fall back to the packs!" ordered Rogers. He knew now that they had only attacked the advanced guard of the enemy. The Rangers jumped, climbed back up the bank and rushed back following their tracks to their dropped packs. As this happened, a few Rangers came running toward Rogers' now left flank. They were the remnants of McDonald's detachment, and they were hotly pursued by droves of the enemy. Also, the enemy had made it to the rear of the retreating Rangers and had begun to pour volleys into their backs. The Rangers loaded and fired as they made it back to their packs, but with great losses. Charles was in the position to see Bulkley, Campbell and Captain Pottinger shot. Fifty men must have dropped in the enemy counter attack. Rogers and the officers who had not been killed rallied the Rangers, and they began a hot fire, loading and firing their muskets as fast as humanly possible.

This was so imposing that the enemy began to fall back. Their skills allowed the Rangers time to reload, and several even ran forward to scalp some of the enemy. The French and Indians again advanced toward the Ranger position. Again, they pushed the French back. This was short lived as the enemy hit the flanks of the Rangers and their front extremely hard. Rogers ordered his men to fall back up the hill behind them. Rogers' flanks fought so hard at this time that the enemy flanks were pushed back to their main body in disorder and at the loss of many Indians.

Once more, the French and Indians attacked with ferocity. Rogers, noticing a large detachment of enemy attempting to out flank his Rangers, ordered Lieutenant Philips and eighteen men to cut them off. Philips and his men got there in time to hold off the enemy.

The enemy must have outnumbered Rogers' force six or seven to one at this time. Noticing that their green coats were making too good of targets, many of the Rangers began to rip off their coats.

Thinking the enemy would attempt to send a party around the other flank, Rogers ordered Lieutenant Crofton and fifteen men to head up the mountain and cover his left. Charles was in this party.

It was now four thirty in the afternoon, and the sun was just beginning to set. Rogers had lost over half of his men, and the enemy was still coming forward, pressing his force. Many of the enemy were less than twenty yards in front of the Rangers, but others now were intermixed with them. Many were now fighting almost hand-to-hand. Rogers now gave the order to break and retreat up the mountain. Rogers had about two-dozen men with him as he climbed up the slopes. Fighting their way to Philips' position, they turned about and gave a deadly volley to the pursuing Indians, dropping at least a dozen and wounding many more. This stopped them for a moment. Rogers and his men did not stay there long as Philips and his men were surrounded by hundreds of Indians and were attempting to surrender. Philips and Rogers came so close that it was heard that Philips stated to the Captain, "If the enemy would give good quarters, I think best we surrender. Otherwise, I will fight while I have one man left to fire a musket!"

"Follow me!" yelled Rogers, and he and his men began to run from the position. Philips and most of his men tried to retreat farther up the mountain with Rogers, but most of Philips' men were cut off. The last thing seen was Philips and his men laying down their weapons. The Indians tied them to trees and barbarously hacked them to pieces!

Rogers and the men with him fought their way to Crofton's position. Indians were everywhere and rushing forth in numbers, overwhelming the Rangers' positions. Rogers, seeing the desperate position they all were in, gave the order to disperse and meet by morning at the rendezvous. "Every man for himself. I'll meet you at the rendezvous!" He shouted as he fired his musket and turned about and ran.

It was like shooting a cannon in a herd of buffalo; men began to scramble in all directions by themselves and in small groups. Rangers took their last shots with their muskets and moved up and around the mountaintop as quickly as their snowshoes could carry them. The only luck at this point was that darkness had fallen. Pringle and Roche, unskilled in snowshoes, could not follow as their bindings were too loose. Charles, Lieutenant Crofton, Mr. Creed and Rogers dashed straight for the peak.

The men were wheezing and snorting like terrified animals, running, crawling and pulling themselves along with every rock, tree and shrub they encountered. Hotly pursuing them were the Indians like a herd of ravenous wolves. Any man who could not continue or was not fast enough was being dragged to the ground and clubbed by the enemy.

Charles felt bullets tearing through his jacket. One knocked off his hat, and another bit him in the meaty flesh of the thigh causing him to twist and fall on his side. As he clawed his way back on his feet, he felt the stinging glance of a native tomahawk on his arm. Charles whirled about, swung his musket catching his assailant between the eyes with the butt of the gun, and rushed forward up the hill. Everywhere men were in the dark, darting about, many continuing to fire muskets with flashes of reddish gold flames in the black night. Charles had lost the others he was running with.

Reaching the crest of the summit, Charles took one quick look outward over the rock cliff and down to the ice below. He knew this would not be an avenue for survival, so he dashed a few rods South of the bald rock cliff. Here along the edge he quickly cut the bindings of the snowshoes and slinging his musket began to slide down into a ravine below. From above, he began to see the flashes of musketry as the enemy reached the summit. Charles reached the ravine and began to climb down using shrubs and small trees that grew in the crevasse. Within a quarter of an hour, he was safe on the ice. He sat there for a few moments trying to gain his composure hidden in a thicket. He slowly reloaded his musket.

There before him coming from the North were three figures jogging along the edge of the ice. Charles prepared for an attack. He brought his musket to his shoulder, cocked it and took careful aim. Just before he pulled the trigger, he could make out the figures as fellow Rangers. It was Waite, Tute and Samuel Cahoon.

Charles stepped out of the thicket and called out quietly, "Ensign Waite, don't shoot; it's Sergeant Nurse." The three men slid to a stop, two of them taking a knee, and the third remaining upright, all taking aim. "Nurse, you're damned lucky I didn't shoot your ass," answered Waite. "Alright, let's keep moving; those heathens will be on us before you know it if they are ambitious enough to try and find a way down this bloody hill in the dark. Keep up with us, Sergeant." The four men rushed to the South, following the lake's coast.

In about an hour, the four men found themselves at the rendezvous. The sleighs were still there, and men were seeing to each other's wounds. It was extremely cold, and there were only a few blankets from the sleighs and marginal food. Most coats and all other blankets had been thrown off at the battle. Rogers sent Cunningham and Scott hurrying back to Fort Edward with a message requesting Colonel Haviland to send assistance to help bring in the wounded. The men sat shivering in pain, cold, hungry and exhausted without fires all night.

The next morning, Rogers took stock of who was present. Using the sleighs, they marched South toward Fort Edward, pulling the wounded that could no longer walk. The march was like dragging themselves to hell. They had no more energy and no provisions or equipment to comfort them in the weather. About six miles North of the ruins of William Henry, Captain Stark and a relief column of Rangers were spied with sleighs filled with blankets, food and medical supplies. The Rangers made it to Hoop Island and started large fires within the security of Stark's guards. Here, they spent the night with warm food and good fires. The next morning, Stark and Rogers brought the entire party into Fort Edward.

It was evening when they arrived, and anyone wounded was taken to the surgeons. It was a pitiful sight with so many men being put through such an ordeal. Many had seen their comrades fall. Most who were now safe at Fort Edward had seen how the savages had given no quarter to their fellow soldiers, hacking them to pieces. Charles was one of the lucky with only a flesh wound to the skin of his right thigh and a cut on his forearm. He was bandaged and given rest and food.

Several days later Charles was called to Rogers hut.

"Sergeant, have a seat," offered Captain Rogers.

"Thank you, sir," replied Charles as he took a seat in the Windsor chair before the desk.

"I have requested you here to offer you an ensign's commission in my Ranger corps. I have been given orders to begin recruiting to form several new companies and also to fill voids left from our battle last week. I have had you on several details and fought along side you at several battles. You have always performed as expected. I also am recommending you a citation for miraculous service at the battle we just returned from. Every man there was under dire straits but performed to the utmost of his abilities. I cannot think of a better man who I would want to have by my side and put my own life in their hands in battle. What say you, Sergeant? Will you take the promotion?" asked Rogers.

"This is truly a great honor, sir. I have always felt honored and accepted in your service. I do believe that your corps is one of the most needed within His Majesty's army. But, I must take my leave and march home now. I have found my redemption, and in doing so I hope that I can return to civilization and my family once again. This does not mean that I may not be returning to the army, but that at this point I am through with it. I must take a rest. After all, I should have a new family when I return. I do thank you, sir," replied Charles.

"Then here are your papers, you are discharged for this campaign and you may return home. There are wagons heading South to Albany within the hour. Here are papers for your passage with them as far as you want to ride. If you ever again want to volunteer or join our corps, you will be welcomed," said Rogers as he handed Charles his papers.

Charles rose and saluted the Captain, who returned the gesture. Charles left the officer's house and collected his belongings from his hut. Time was wasting. Charles hurried to the stable to ride along with the wagons heading to Albany.

HOME AT LAST

The train of wagons departed the fort and headed South along the wagon road. There were no mishaps along the way other than a broken wheel that the wagoners replaced in less than two hours. Once at Albany, Charles switched to a sleigh heading East into Massachusetts delivering dispatches to General Winslow in Boston.

The weather was very cold, and the travel was swift along the frozen road. Snow fell, and on the fourth day a blinding blizzard all but stopped the sleigh. About an hour before dark, they ventured upon the Hall Tavern in Deerfield and decided they had gone far enough for the day.

The next morning, Charles and the sleigh driver ventured out just before dawn. The snow had stopped and the travel now was better, and they glided quickly East. By late afternoon they had reached Boston, and Charles obtained travel on a cart heading North up the coast toward Salisbury. Charles and the cart driver traveled all night, and by afternoon they were passing Newbury. Charles bid him farewell and began the walk to Amesbury along the Merrimack River.

It wasn't long until the sun had set, and Charles was finding his way by moonlight. His feet crunched on the frozen ground as he walked along the road. On his left was the Powow, the river he had grown up on and the source of his income as a boat builder in Amesbury. Along both sides of the road rose tall oaks that had been there since Charles' grandparent's time and before. Many of their limbs creaked and cracked in the bitter breeze. Charles shivered a little to shake off the temperature. Periodically along the route, a candle lantern glowed in the distance to the right from a farmhouse or barn.

It was very late when Charles made it to his parents' farm. There were no signs of them being awake, but he had to just stand there for a few moments and reminisce. The saltbox house had been in the family for several generations, and all the Nurse family had been born there. Charles had learned to fire his first fowler in the woods behind and had cared for his father's cattle and tended the crops. He breathed deep and could almost smell his mother's cooking.

Charles continued on the wagon road, and when he reached the edge of the field to the West of his parents, he came to the lane leading to his home. The weathered clapboard house was well kept and quaint. To the West stood his out buildings where he had spent many hours working on his farm and tending his animals. As Charles walked up the lane, he noticed that the curtains Mary had sewn were still hanging in the windows, making the place much more suitable for a family than before. It was late, and Charles knew the door would be bolted. He remembered that the latch on the wood box never worked, and that if the box was not full he could crawl through the outdoor lid into the storage box in the kitchen. Charles was right, and he wiggled his way into the kitchen. The room was still warm compared to the cold of the outdoors, but there were only coals left in the hearth. He knelt down to work on the fire.

"Oh, Lord Jehovah, Charles Nurse," whispered Sarah. Charles had not reckoned disturbing Mary's mother. She was standing in the doorway between the great room and the kitchen holding Charles' fowler. Charles quickly held both hands out in front of himself and pleaded, "Sarah, don't shoot, put the damned gun down and don't wake them up."

Sarah set the fowler in the corner and walked over to Charles and gave him a big hug. "It is wonderful to see you. We have been so worried. You must go to Mary. We can talk in the morning."

Charles rekindled the fire in the kitchen and went into the great room and did the same in that hearth. He quietly tiptoed into the bedchamber.

Inside he could instantly smell Mary's aroma. He stood there for a moment. Then Charles walked past his grandfather's highboy and rubbed his hand across its smooth finish as he passed. Charles stood at the foot of the bed for a moment. Mary lay there and wrapped up in swaddling and tucked up in the crook of her arm was a baby. Tears began to stream down Charles' cheeks. Suddenly, everything that he had lived through was far away and only he, Mary and the baby were real.

Charles quietly took a nightshirt from the highboy and removed his shirt, hose and breeches and slipped it over his head.

He walked over and slid between the covers. Mary let out a terrifying scream and instantly swung the fist of her left arm into Charles' stomach. He jumped from the bed and Mary yelled, "Get out, no, no, get out of here!" The baby began to wail, frightened by the commotion.

"It's alright, my dear," Charles said calmly. "I have come home to you. Didn't you get my letter?" quizzed Charles.

"Oh, my stars, of course I did, but I certainly didn't expect your cold feet to jump in bed with me and Samuel in the middle of the night," geared Mary.

"You mean I have a son!" said Charles stunned.

"You most certainly do. Do you want to hold him?" offered Mary.

Mary handed Charles the baby as he sat on the edge of the bed. "You named him after my grandfather," is all that Charles could say. Charles pulled the blanket off the boy. He bounced the baby slightly and comforted him, and the child soon quit crying. Samuel was a healthy boy just over six months old and with a reddish ting to his hair. He was big and strong and cooed as his father held him.

The three spent the rest of the evening getting reconnected and enjoying each other.

The next morning, Charles woke late; it was nearly eight. Mary had risen with Samuel early, and her and Sarah began to fix a big meal. Enoch, Charles' fourteen-year-old brother, had come over to tend to the animals for Mary. Learning that Charles had arrived home, he had rushed home and retrieved Caleb and Margaret.

Charles had not felt so comfortable for months. The room was warm, and he was well rested. He slowly stretched and yawned attempting to wake himself. Charles slid his legs over the bed and looked around the room in the daylight streaming through the window. The room was flooded with a reddish glow from the checked curtains. Charles heard a soft chirping noise from beside him, and he turned around to find his son, Samuel, lying on the bed. Charles quickly put on his britches, shirt, and hose and slid on his house shoes. He had not felt them on his feet since last spring. Charles bent over and kissed his son on the head and picked him up. Cradling Samuel to his chest, Charles walked into the great room and back into the kitchen area.

His family welcomed Charles when he walked into the kitchen. Caleb was first and raised his hands to the sky and prayed. "Praise Jehovah, you are home and all in one piece. I have prayed for this day." Caleb hugged Charles.

Mary walked over and gave Charles a peck on the cheek and took Samuel from him.

"I must sit," said Margaret. "Oh, my son, you look so thin. You must never go again," Margaret said sternly. Charles walked to his mother who had placed herself in a chair. Sarah brought Margaret a damp cloth for her head.

"Mother, I have often thought of you and father and how I was serving to keep you safe. I prayed to see you again," reassured Charles. Margaret hugged and kissed Charles.

"I've been reading the papers looking for your name. I knew you could not have been killed. You're too good for those Frenchmen to kill you," Enoch said fistedly.

"I'm home now, brother. It was the Indians I was worried about," replied Charles as the two brothers shook hands and embraced.

"Indians, real savages! I heard that many of you had been captured. I also read about them scalping, hacking and doing terrible things to our men; is it true?" asked Enoch.

Charles was taken by surprise by his emotions about this question. He did not answer and opened the back door of his house and walked out; he could not stay there and be questioned about what he had gone through. He walked through the remnants of the herb garden and opened the gate and walked to the barn. His father followed him.

"Charles, I understand some of what you are feeling. There is no way Enoch knows how what he asks brings back memories you wish not to revisit. I too, as you know, went through war, and as you know I rarely have spoken of it. I cannot imagine what you have witnessed being a captive of the Indians and a prisoner of war," reassured Caleb. He hesitated and put a hand on Charles' shoulder. "Come on back in. We can work it out. You need to be there for your family now. There will be plenty of healing to be done, but let's begin by going back inside."

Charles didn't say anything. He reached down and picked up a shovel leaning against the manger and began to beat the wooden wall of the stall. With the third strike the scoop broke off the handle, which sent it flying across the barn, but Charles continued. Finally, he dropped the shovel handle. He was out of breath and put his hands on his knees and tried to catch his breath. Caleb knew to give him his distance. After several minutes, Charles had calmed down enough to talk.

"Father, I have seen things, terrible things. I witnessed men and women killed and scalped. I was stripped and painted like a savage and forced to eat the flesh of another man by the savages. I was beaten and nearly starved and forced to do their bidding. There are many other things too, but I will never speak of them." Charles took a deep breath before continuing. "There were times when they accepted me and took me into their family. I was taken care of then. But no matter how nice they were, I never forgot that I must make it home."

Caleb put his hand on Charles' shoulder again and said, "Let's go in now." The two men walked back inside.

Once inside, Mary handed the two men steeping pewter mugs of hot tea. Charles cupped his hands around it, blew on the hot liquid and took a sip. Mary leaned over and whispered in Charles' ear. "My love, there is no need for me to know what you have seen or done. I am just content to have you as my husband. I will never question you." She then gave him a kiss.

Charles was surprised; this type of open affection was somewhat rare. Margaret and Sarah were slightly taken back. They blushed and looked at each other. Caleb tapped himself on the belly and told the family, "Very well. Ladies, if we are ready to eat lets be seated." Everyone took their seats, Charles at the head, and Mary at the other end of the large trestle table. On one side of the table sat Margaret and Caleb and opposite them sat Enoch. "Charles, it is with great thanks that we have our son home once again. Would you please do us the honor and lead us in the blessing," suggested Caleb.

Charles was nervous and placed both hands on the table before him. He closed his eyes and bowed his head. Everyone became silent as he spoke. "Lord Jehovah, we are gathered here before you and thank You for the chance to bow our heads in Your reverence." Charles hesitated and sighed. "Lord, I must take a moment and thank You for bringing me back to my family. I have followed You and Your chosen leaders to fight our enemies. I must be frank. I have seen hell, the site of men being slaughtered and maimed and the atrocities that were inflicted on us by the hellhounds from the fare West, all this under the knowledge of their French officers. I have seen, and I have done terrible things. I ask my family to never ask me to talk about them. I only ask my family and You, Jehovah, to forgive me in my sins committed in the name of war." Charles now paused and took Caleb's hand and Enoch's in his other hand and prayed further. "Jehovah, I am home now and this is the past. I thank you for the peace of having this wonderful family. I thank you as well for blessing us with my son, Samuel, and making him so healthy. Lord, we thank you for this fine feast that Mary, Sarah and Mother have prepared for us and thank you for this season, and spring will begin any day. If I may, Lord, bless our work as we prepare our fields. Allow us to be prosperous and continue to bless us with your bounty as we worship you, Jehovah." Charles once more hesitated. "Lord, ours is a proud family. We have marched when you asked for the name of this Holy War against the French. We have sacrificed a brother and son and a father and friend for this cause. We have all personally sacrificed in many other ways too. Lord, I ask you that we may swiftly bring an end to this terrible conflict. But Jehovah, if you see it necessary again to call one of the men of our family into your service in order for others to remain free and safe here in the Powow Valley, then let it be me you use as your right hand to smite Your enemies." Charles opened his eyes and concluded. "Lord, thank you for so many wonders and thank you for Your continued love, A-men."

The family was cheerful and filled their plates with the wonderful meal. Conversation was pleasant, but no one asked Charles more of his experiences. Samuel brought smiles to everyone during the meal and was passed around and fed with glee by everyone.

Everyone seemed to have something in the back of their minds though. It stemmed from Charles' prayer. Would he return to the army? Would he volunteer to march with the Boston Regiments? Would he leave his family once more? His odds were lessoning of returning home.

The next few weeks saw spring and the planting of the crops. Families across the colony rejoiced with the presence of their loved ones. But, lurking in the discussions in the meetinghouse, shops and tavern was that of the next campaign.

Would Massachusetts-Bay offer levies to fight once more? Would Charles volunteer?